Happy Cooking!

GARY RHODES'
Sweet Dreams

GARY RHODES'
Sweet Dreams

Hodder & Stoughton

For my wife, Jenny, who's always feeding me –

SWEET DREAMS

Acknowledgements
Borra Garson
Wayne Tapsfield and the team at *city rhodes*
Gardner Merchant
Jo' Pratt
Lynne Meikle, Phil Richardson and Isy Foss
Laura Brockbank, Hazel Orme, Martin Lovelock and Sian Irvine

A very special thank you to my pastry chef, Jane Huffer,
one of the most talented I've had the pleasure to work with and
without whom this book would not have been possible.

First published in 1998 by Hodder & Stoughton
A division of Hodder Headline PLC

10 9 8 7 6 5 4 3 2 1

British Library Cataloguing in Publication Data

ISBN: 0 340 71239 2

Photography by Sian Irvine
Designed by Lovelock & Co

Printed and bound in Great Britain by Butler & Tanner Ltd.

Hodder and Stoughton
A division of Hodder Headline PLC · 338 Euston Road · London NW1 3BH

Contents

Introduction

'Although from Puddings to Pastry is but a step, it requires a higher degree of art to make the one than to make the other. Indeed, pastry is one of the most important branches of the culinary science. It unceasingly occupies itself with ministering pleasure to the sight as well as to the taste; with erecting graceful monuments, miniature fortresses, and all kinds of architectural imitations, composed of the sweetest and most agreeable products of all climates and countries.'

These words, taken from Mrs Isabella Beeton's *Book of Household Management*, 1884, show, and explain, how there has been little change in thought or feeling about puddings and desserts in the last 130-odd years. In fact, I'm quite sure that this idea was around for many years before Mrs Beeton expressed it. There's often a building process involved in creating puddings, desserts, afters, not always the building of towers, monuments or fortresses but of flavours and textures. Pastry-making is indeed one of the most important branches of culinary science. Whatever the filling, a tart, pie or flan will always stay in the First Division and never make the Premiership class if the pastry is not right. It needs soft work with care and attention. An extra five, ten minutes, and the science works.

Albert and Michel Roux are the chefs I most admire. These men shared their passion for food and their culinary skills with other chefs and those who visit their restaurants and read their books. Michel is probably the most skilful patissier in Britain. In his books, he writes of his love of making simple pastry. He tells us that even when it's raw it can titillate his taste-buds, that working with the finger-tips has a very sensual feel. Pastry must be kneaded carefully so that it remains supple, then rolled quickly and evenly to avoid bruising it. Have you ever worried about bruising your pastry? It's only when you think about it that you know exactly what he means, that bruised pastry has been overworked, overstretched and toughened. It's this sensitivity that I try to apply to all my food, not overchurning ice-cream, which gives a crumbly texture, but instead working it to a rich thick cream that just melts.

Many dishes are built from individual components, most of which can be made in advance, but where possible I've given suggestions and alternatives to save you making everything from scratch. The idea is to make sure that it's not just the pastry that doesn't get bruised but you too!

The book has been put together as one long chapter. It was difficult to break it down and although I got carried away with some subjects, I just wanted you to read on. Each recipe carries its own introduction which tells you something about the dish and will hopefully give your tastebuds those tingly feelings.

The ice-creams really excited me: I have turned classic dishes almost upside down! Take the Apple Pie, for example: you break through a light but crisp sweet pastry to find a rich ice-cream just starting to melt and chunky apple base. It's a dream. And the ice-cream is made with tinned custard and bought apple purée.

The idea of this book was not to try to turn everyone into a professional patissier but to give pleasure with puddings. You'll find at least one for every occasion. There are the à la carte style desserts: they will take a little time – like the British Pudding Plate on page 20 or the Pear Plate on page 146 – but are just the thing for that special dinner. For Sunday Lunch you might try Steamed Bakewell Pudding (page 71), or Apple and Almond Bake (page 27). At Afternoon Teas, serve Gypsy Tart (page 53), or American Cheesecake (page 154). Or if you're in a rush, try something fast and easy like Lemon Posset (page 81) and Iced Sweet Fool (page 167).

Presentation of puddings is important and I always go for simplicity. Let it show its ingredients to their best, and avoid excess. However, with puddings, there's always room to show other skills, colour, textures and, hopefully, flavour too. Simple chocolate pencils and shavings can change the face of a dish. Try making a small piping-bag from greaseproof paper and decorate plates with chocolate or icing – a message or pattern gives a great effect. Or pipe a tear-drop and fill it with fruit coulis beside the main dessert: it looks stunning. So do shaped tuiles or brandy snaps. Petits fours are another feature – there are plenty to choose from, but just one done well can be enough.

There are also stories about sugar: Tate & Lyle, a household name and part of our history, have been creating sweet products for us for over a century, Lyle's Golden Syrup probably being the most famous. And we take a look at chocolate too. Both sugar and chocolate, the products we use today, amaze me. They come from plants that were discovered thousands of years ago and have been transformed through technology into everyday sprinkling and munching.

This book is here to make puddings approachable and enjoyable to you. The recipes to start that tingling. The pictures to create that dribbling. The making to finish with eating.

In other words, giving you ... **Sweet Dreams**

Gary Rhodes

Hints and Tips

This section contains notes on products, tips, hints and details. Some are obvious, others odd. However you see them, they're worth a read.

Fromage blanc and Fromage frais
Fromage blanc is a soft unripened cheese, usually made from skimmed cow's milk with a culture.

Fromage frais is fromage blanc, beaten to a smooth consistency.

Both contain between zero and 8 per cent fat, unless they have been enriched with cream. Fromage frais can replace yoghurt in ice-creams, mousses, etc.

Crème fraîche
In France, chefs use crème fraîche to finish sweet and savoury sauces. Double or clotted creams contain an average 48 per cent fat, crème fraîche just 30 per cent. Crème fraîche is made by pasteurising milk before the cream has formed. The milk is then separated into cream and skimmed milk. The cream is pasteurised again, to give it extra shelf life, and selected lactic cultures are added to give it acidity.

Sour Cream
Single or double cream that has been treated with a souring culture and contains approximately 20 per cent butterfat. You can make your own sour cream by adding a few drops of lemon juice to either double or whipping cream.

Yoghurt
Low-fat or skimmed milk treated with a culture of selected lactic ferments. The butterfat content is between 8 and 10 per cent, making yoghurt a healthy eating and cooking product.

Ice-creams
The double cream used in any of these recipes can be replaced with whipping cream for less fat. Sour cream can be used to replace crème fraîche and yoghurt.

Peeling apples
Use downward movements, from stalk to base: this keeps the shape of the apple. Peeling round results in an uneven surface.

Weights and Measures

All recipes are written to metric. They can be converted to imperial by using the tables below. Do not combine metric and imperial.

Liquid Conversions		Solid Weight Conversions	
Metric	**Imperial**	**Metric**	**Imperial**
15 ml	½ fl oz	5 g	¼ oz
20 ml	⅔ fl oz	10 g	½ oz
30 ml	1 fl oz	20 g	¾ oz
50 ml	1⅔ fl oz	25 g	1 oz
60 ml	2 fl oz	50 g	2 oz
90 ml	3 fl oz	75 g	3 oz
100 ml	3⅓ fl oz	100 g	4 oz
150 ml	5 fl oz (¼ pint)	150 g	5 oz
200 ml	6⅔ fl oz	175 g	6 oz
250 ml	8 fl oz	200 g	7 oz
300 ml	10 fl oz (½ pint)	225 g	8 oz
500 ml	16⅔ fl oz	350 g	12 oz
600 ml	20 fl oz (1 pint)	450 g	1 lb
1 litre	1¾ pints		

Cherries

Morello cherries are small and extremely bitter. In France, they are known as *Griottes*. *Griottine* cherries, which are featured in several recipes, are the *Griottes* that have been steeped in alcohol. The world famous Black Forest Gâteau (Schwarzwälder Kirschtorte) was always made with Morello cherries flavoured with *Kirschwasser*, a Black Forest version of cherry brandy.

Genoise

A basic sponge cake used in many gâteaux and desserts. The name, they say, derived from the town of its birth: Genoa.

Eggs

All eggs are large.

Tablespoon

My tablespoon measurements are 15 g for solids and 15 ml for liquids.

Teaspoon

My teaspoon measurements are 5 g for solids and 5 ml for liquids.

Chocolate

I recommend Lindt chocolate for all recipes that require either plain or bitter chocolate. Supermarkets also supply their own brand of good, high-cocoa-solids chocolate.

Sugar

Tate & Lyle – is there any other?

Blind-baking pastry

Line the tin/ring/case with the pastry and leave it to rest. Now line it with baking paper along with baking beans or rice and bake. **Note:** When blind-baking pastry cases, it is best to leave the excess pastry hanging over the rim. Once it is cooked, trim off the edges and you have a perfectly neat, even finish.

Gas gun

These powerful butane gas canisters are available from almost any hardware store. Read the instructions carefully before use: gas guns are not conventionally used in the kitchen. Obviously, they should not be used by children.

Meringue

Egg whites increase in volume by up to seven times when whipped, provided all utensils used are spotlessly clean, because they contain so much protein – 11 per cent – which forms tiny filaments that stretch on beating, and incorporate air in minute bubbles. They set to form a puffed-up structure.

Vanilla

Vanilla is found in tropical rainforests. The pods are picked when they are unripe and yellow. They are allowed to mature to a deep dark brown, but are not dried. When you purchase vanilla pods, they will have a ribbed soft texture. They can be kept in an airtight jar with your caster sugar, which should be used mostly in cooking. If you continue to top up the jar, you'll always have vanilla sugar.

Baking parchment

The finest cooking paper, used for lining cake-tins and for placing under either sweet or savoury items as they cook. Meringues will not stick to parchment.

Greaseproof paper

Used in much the same way as parchment. However, greaseproof is best buttered or oiled to guarantee non-stick.

Quenelle

A quenelle describes the neat oval shape achieved between two spoons of mousses, creams, chocolates and other soft, workable substances. It is classically applied to fish or meat forcemeat. The spoons should be slightly warmed so that the mousse will fall away from them easily.

Scroll
Described in the *Concise English Dictionary* as 'a decorative carving or moulding resembling a scroll'. I can't better that!

Sabayon
A thick creamy froth, created classically from whisking egg yolks with sugar and flavouring, such as sweet white wine, in a bowl over simmering water. Sabayon can also be made in an electric mixer, but the bowl should be warmed first.

Gluten
An elastic substance that assists in trapping CO_2 in a dough. On ripening, the gluten becomes extensible so that expansion can take place without loss of gas (your cake won't rise). During baking, the gluten coagulates and, with other proteins, forms the structure of bread or cake.

Fruity Seasons

Most fruits are now available throughout the year, which has its advantages, but you can't beat good Scottish raspberries and English strawberries in season. This list tells you what is in season and when. Imported fruits are often delicious, but if it's British and it's in season, use it!

Apples		**Cherries**		**Gooseberries**	July–Aug
Bramley's cooking apple	Nov–March	Morello	Aug	**Redcurrants**	July–Aug
		Early Rivers	June		
Cox's Orange Pippin	Oct–Jan	Stella	July	**Plums**	Aug–Sept
Discovery	Aug–Sept	**Blackberries**	July–Sept	**Peaches**	July–Aug
Golden Delicious	Nov–Feb	**Tayberries**	July–Aug	**Apricots**	late Aug
Granny Smith	Jan–April	**Loganberries**	July–Aug	**Nectarines**	early Sept
		Raspberries	July–Sept	**Figs**	Aug–Sept
Pears					
Conference	Oct–Nov	**Strawberries**	May–Aug	**Tangerines**	Dec
Comice	Nov–Dec				
Williams	Sept	**Blackcurrants**	early–late July	**Rhubarb**	Dec–June

Soft Flour
Flour containing a weak gluten.

Strong Flour
Flour containing a strong, stable gluten.

Cochineal
A red food dye, called carmine, used to create a pink colour in sponges, mousses, etc. (and to colour half of the sponge mix in the Battenberg Cake page xx). The name comes from the cochineal insect, a species of beetle, originally used to form the dye. The female insects were collected after they had been fertilized by the male and before the complete development of the eggs. They were either put in an oven on metal sheets for a few moments or blanched in boiling water and dried. After pressing the carmine colour was collected. Don't worry, nowadays cochineal is artificially produced. It's the *Beatles* who will never leave us!

Bread and Butter Pudding – as you've never seen it before!

Tea strainer
Brilliant to use as a sprinkler for icing sugar and cocoa powder. Half fill it and tap it gently to give a light dusting.

Caramelised Melba Toasts
So simple, so good, I just had to mention them here. They are excellent served as a homemade biscuit with ice-cream (as above). I've given lots of recipes for different-flavoured tuiles and brandy-snaps that are hard to beat, but they take more time.

   Toast medium-sliced bread on both sides. Then remove the crusts and split the slice through the middle. Scrape away the crumbs and cut each piece into two triangles. Dust heavily with icing sugar and sit them at the bottom of a grill on a low setting. The sugar will slowly caramelise and the bread will toast. Once it is golden with burnt tinges of sugar, your Melbas are ready.

Cylinder Ring Moulds
Several sizes of stainless steel ring moulds are used throughout this book. These can be found in kitchen or department stores. Don't worry about finding the exact size ring, something close will do just as well. Any cold dishes requiring these rings can be made in plastic equivalents. These, of course, can be 'homemade' using drain piping found in your local DIY store.

Sugar: The Base for Sweet Dreams

Sugar has a very long history. It is not known from where it originated, but it is thought to have been first used five thousand years ago in the Polynesian islands of the Pacific Ocean, where it was discovered that the stalks of the giant grass we call sugar-cane contained a sweet liquid that could be used in food preparation.

Sugar was first taken to the coastal areas of India and, for centuries, spread no further. It was in 510 BC that Darius, the Persian Emperor, arrived to conquer the Indian sub-continent and found that a plant substance was being used to sweeten food. The Persians had used only honey until then, and they named sugar-cane 'the reed which gives honey without bees'! Next, Alexander the Great, in the fourth century AD, was conquering parts of Western Asia and took with him what he called the 'Sacred Reed'. Ancient Greece and Rome started to import sugar as a luxury product and a medicine. In the seventh century AD, Arabs invaded Persia and brought away the sugar-cane plant.

It soon reached other countries, including Egypt, *Rhodes*, Cyprus, North Africa (Morocco and Tunisia), Southern Spain and Syria. In the fifteenth century, the Arabs introduced it to the rest of Spain and Portugal. It proved a highly profitable product, and new places were needed to grow it.

In 1493, Christopher Columbus took sugar-cane to the Caribbean island of Santo Domingo for trial plantings, where it flourished in the hot sunshine, good fertile soil and heavy rainfall. This was to create a new history for sugar-cane. It grew faster in the West Indies than anywhere else in the world. Farmers from Britain, France and Holland made the most of the discovery and developed plantations in Brazil, Cuba, Mexico and the West Indies, for export. Sugar farming was so profitable a business that people spoke of sugar as 'white gold'. In the fourteenth century, it was sold at two shillings a pound, which today equals £44 a pound! Sugar was pure luxury.

In the mid-seventeenth century, Britain won Jamaica and part of the West Indies from Spain, and by the middle of the eighteenth century, there were 120 sugar-refining factories in the UK producing up to 30,000 tonnes of cane sugar each year. The British government taxed sugar heavily, until in 1874, the Prime Minister, William Gladstone, removed the tax and sugar became affordable to nearly everyone.

Sugar is sucrose, which is accumulated in the tissue fluids of a tropical reed (sugar-cane) that can grow up to 5 metres high. To maximise its yield, the plant needs an average temperature of 24°C (75°F), along with about

2 metres of rainfall per year. Consequently, it can only be successfully grown in the latitude zone between 25° north and south of the Equator. Each plantation can run for approximately seven seasons. The plants need 11 to 18 months to mature. Most are cut down around their twelfth month. The roots are left in the ground to grow for the next season: this is called 'ratooning'.

After cutting/cropping, the plant deteriorates quickly, so it is crushed in the country in which it is grown. At the factory, it is cleaned of stones and earth, etc., then shredded to break the hard rind and expose the inner core, in which the sugar is found. The next process is to crush it between rollers and spray with hot water to release the sugar. This liquid is then clarified and the mixture evaporated and crystallised. The resulting 'masse' is spun in high speed centrifugal machines, similar to a spin-drier, to separate the sugar crystals (raw cane sugar) from the residual syrup (cane molasses). It is absolutely essential to obtain the sugar in a crystalline form as cane juice quickly ferments and goes off.

The raw cane sugar (brown in colour) is now in a stable form, containing up to 99 per cent sucrose (pure sugar) and is subsequently shipped abroad. Once in Britain, the sugar is further refined. Most of the 'impurities' (non sugars) in the raw sugars end up in molasses. The raw sugar consists of relatively pure sugar crystals surrounded by a syrupy film. The first stage of processing is to remove the surface syrup. Raw sugar is mixed with a hot refinery syrup to soften the film and then passed into centrifugal machines, which separate the syrups from the crystals. The crystals may still contain some 'impurities'. They are now dissolved in water and the syrup undergoes a further clarification and filtration similar to the processing in the raw sugar factory. This removes final insoluble matter. Some colour may also be removed by passing over adsorbants. The resulting liquor is then boiled at low temperatures in vacuum pans.

At the appropriate stage a little fine icing sugar is added to stimulate crystallisation. When the crystals have grown to the size required they are separated from the mother syrup by centrifugation as before. Not all of the sugar is recovered in one boiling so the syrup is reboiled and crystallised several times, but with each boiling the concentration of the residual non-sugars is increased. The sugar is totally refined and from the remaining syrup and intermediate syrups from the refining process are produced golden syrup, treacle, brown sugars and molasses.

Sugar varieties

Granulated Sugar: the most popular, all-purpose sugar with a crystal size of approximately 0.65 mm.

Caster Sugar: produced more or less as for granulated, but finishing with a finer crystal size of approximately 0.3 mm.

Icing Sugar: made from granulated that is then ground and blended with an anti-caking agent to maintain its free-flowing characteristics.

Demerara Sugar: originally from the Demerara district of Guyana, but is now produced in a number of raw-sugar-producing countries. It is a raw cane sugar with golden crystals. Its characteristic flavour and texture come from the molasses surrounding each crystal.

Brown Soft Sugars: from light to dark with different depths of flavour and colour, resulting from the minerals and organic non-sugars of cane molasses surrounding each crystal.

Sweet strengths

All the different forms of sucrose, whether raw or refined, hold the same degree of sweetness. It is when they are eaten dry that they all give a different strength. Granulated, being the larger crystal, dissolves more slowly, building up a sweetness, while icing sugar, in contrast, gives immediate rich sweetness that disappears quickly. When we eat sucrose, our metabolism turns the sugar into carbon dioxide and water, thus releasing energy.

Tate & Lyle

Sir Henry Tate (1819–99) and Abram Lyle III (1800–91) owned sugar refineries on separate sites, no more than a mile and a half apart. When Tate moved from Liverpool and Lyle from Greenock, in the mid 1880s, they took up sites on the Thames, still used by Tate & Lyle Sugars today. Sir Henry Tate became famous for producing sugar in cube form, an idea he had seen in Germany, and to which he bought the rights. Abram Lyle brought golden syrup with him. Many other sugar products were also being produced at both of their refineries but it has been said that the two men never actually met! For it was not until 1921, long after they had both passed away, that the two companies became one and Tate & Lyle was born.

Henry Tate gave handsomely to hospitals, schools and institutions. He was heralded as 'one of the munificent merchant princes whose name takes an honourable place in the national record' and the legacy for which he is best known, the National Gallery of British Art, better known as the Tate Gallery in London, was built in 1897.

Today, Tate & Lyle's Thames refinery produces the largest amount of refined cane sugar in the world, operating at up to 160 tonnes per hour and processing over a million tonnes per year.

So remember, smile, it's **Sweet Dreams**!

British Pudding Plate

This pudding is everyone's Sweet Dream. Just imagine a plate with three mini great British classics looking at you – and the combinations are endless. Here, though, I've suggested you try Bread and Butter Pudding Ice-cream with Caramelised Melba Toasts, Open Apple Pie with Sauce Anglaise, and Rhubarb Trifle, which offer a selection of different textures and flavours, with pastry, fruit and ice-cream. Obviously there's work involved with so many dishes on one plate, but it's worth every minute! You can use each recipe as a complete dish in its own right: it's not essential to make them all!

Here are some other Great British Dishes which can be made in smaller portions and moulds to suit the British Pudding Plate:

Steamed Treacle Sponge (page 69); Sticky Toffee Pudding (page 76); Jaffa Cake Pudding (page 122–3); Warm Black Forest Gateau (page 150); Gypsy Tart (page 53); Apple Pie Ice-cream (page 97–8); Hot Pear Puffs (page 138); Crème Brûlées (page 47); Bread and Butter Pudding (pages 38-9); Mini Lemon Meringue Tarts (page 176).

Note: The presentation of the British Pudding Plate featured here is shown in the photograph on page xx.

Rhubarb Trifle

Serves 6–8 in Great British
  Pudding Plate, *or* 4

1 x Swiss roll tin, lined with
  buttered greaseproof paper *or*
  1 x 15–18 cm cake tin for a
  large trifle

For the sponge
– or 1 bought sponge cake
2 eggs
60 g caster sugar
60 g plain flour

Preheat the oven to 200°C/400°F/Gas Mark 6.

Make the sponge. Whisk the eggs and caster sugar together in a bowl over simmering water until the mixture is light, creamy and has doubled in volume. Remove it from the heat and continue to whisk until it is at room temperature. Fold in the sieved flour very gently and spread in the tin. Bake for 10–12 minutes until just firm. Remove from the oven and leave to cool before turning out. If making one large trifle cake, then cook the sponge mixture in a 15–18 cm round cake tin. (The sponge can be halved, freezing one for your next trifle!!). The Swiss roll tin cake base can now be cut into 6–8 rings, using the individual moulds.

To prepare the sherry syrup, bring the stock syrup to a simmer with the sherry. Remove from the heat. This can now be spooned in intervals on to the sponge bases (or base, if a large trifle is being made) to moisten.

Cut the rhubarb into 1–2 cm pieces. Reduce the oven temperature to 180°C/350°F/Gas Mark 4 and place the rhubarb pieces on a baking tray, each standing up. Sprinkle with the caster sugar and bake for approximately 8–10 minutes until the rhubarb is just tender. Pour off any juices and reserve for the jelly. Allow the fruit to cool.

To make the jelly, allow the gelatine leaves to soak in cold water. After a few minutes the leaves will become soft and can be lightly squeezed to remove excess water. Warm the rhubarb juices and add the squeezed gelatine. Lightly stir and the gelatine will quickly dissolve, strain through a sieve and leave to cool. The cooked rhubarb pieces can now be arranged on top of the soaked sponge and, when the jelly has cooled to a thick and almost setting consistency, spoon it on top of the rhubarb.

For the sherry syrup
100 ml stock syrup, page 188
2 tablespoons of sweet sherry

For the rhubarb
500 g rhubarb
150 g sugar

For the rhubarb jelly
1½ –2 leaves gelatine
200 ml rhubarb juice (from cooked rhubarb)

For the custard, soak the gelatine in cold water. Bring the milk, double cream and split vanilla pod to the boil. Beat together the yolks and sugar. Whisk the hot milk and cream on to the eggs, place the bowl over a pan of water and return to a low heat, stirring constantly, until thickened and coating the back of a spoon. Remove from the heat, squeeze any excess water from the gelatine and add to the custard. Stir until the gelatine has dissolved, then strain the custard. Leave to cool, and chill until almost setting. At this point, spoon the custard on top of the rhubarb leaving a 4–5 mm space from the top to leave room for the whipped cream. Refrigerate to set.

This complete method also applies if you are making a large trifle.

There are several ways of finishing this dish for presentation. It's not necessary to spread the cream on top before removing the trifles from the rings, which can be achieved in two ways: either carefully release the edges

For the custard
160 ml milk
1 vanilla pod
3 egg yolks
60 g caster sugar
1 vanilla pod
170 ml double cream
1 leaf gelatine
85–120 ml double *or* whipping cream, for topping

with a warmed small knife before lifting off the mould; or warm around the ring (provided it's metal!) with a gas gun, then with a cloth just lift off the ring for a perfect finish. The lightly whipped cream can now be spooned or piped, using a 5 mm–1 cm tube, on top, leaving a small peak.

Another method, and one of my favourites, is to dust the cream heavily with icing sugar and then 'grill-mark' with heated skewers. The grill look changes the whole feel of a trifle. I serve thick cream separately for you to help yourselves.

You'll find a photograph of the large grill-marked trifle on page 21.

Bread and Butter Pudding Ice-cream

Serves 6–8

For the cream
250 ml whipping cream
250 ml milk
25 g raisins
25 g sultanas
1 vanilla pod, split
¼ teaspoon ground nutmeg
   (preferably fresh)

For the crumbs
100 g fresh white breadcrumbs
40 g Demerara sugar

For the custard
6 egg yolks
50 g caster sugar

Caramelised Melba Toasts (page 13)

Bread and Butter Pudding is a total experience, one I will never tire of! Even so, I've been threatening to turn the original idea into ice-cream for some time and the results have been worth waiting for. The Caramelised Melba Toasts represent the crispy glazed topping of the hot pudding. The ice-cream for the Pudding Plate has simply been scooped but you'll see how good it looks set in a ring if you turn to the photograph on page 13.

Preheat the oven to 180°C/350°F/Gas Mark 4.

Bring all of the ingredients for the cream to a simmer. Remove from the heat and allow to infuse for 20–30 minutes.

Meanwhile, mix the crumbs with the Demerara sugar and spread on a baking sheet. Roast for approximately 10 minutes, then remove the tray from the oven. The crumbs and sugar will have begun to solidify: break them down again into crumbs and return to the oven for a further 5 minutes. Remove from the oven and break to a crumble. Leave to one side.

Make the custard. Cream together the egg yolks and sugar. Remove the vanilla pod from the cream mixture and strain the cream on to the yolks. Keep the fruit to one side. Whisk the egg mixture with the cream and return it to the saucepan, or bowl over simmering water, and cook the custard over a low heat until it thickens and coats the back of a spoon. Add the reserved fruit and allow to cool. Once cool, stir the crumbs into the mix. Now churn the ice-cream in an ice-cream maker for 20–25 minutes until it has thickened and increased in volume. Pour it into a bowl and allow it to finish setting in the freezer.

To serve, sit a triangle of Caramelised Melba Toast (see page 13) on top of a scroll of the ice-cream. You could also trickle a little Sauce Anglaise (see page 191) around it, to represent the custard that flows out of a baked Bread and Butter Pudding when cut.

Note: The rings used for the individual ice-cream are 7.5 x 3.5 cm.

This ice-cream can also be made without an ice-cream machine. Once ready for churning, place the mix in a large bowl and freeze until well thickened. Now whip to keep a blended consistency, refreeze and repeat this process every 15–20 minutes until almost set. Leave to freeze completely.

Pressed Open Apple Pie

Apple pie and custard is another British Great. This one holds all of the pie flavours, but for the Pudding plate, I thought we could present it differently, showing all of those flavours. If the rings/moulds are unavailable, a small apple pie can be made, filling it with the caramelised apples from this recipe.

Metal or plastic moulds can be used to build the apples. Plastic will obviously be in preference for re-heating through the microwave.

Note: Plastic moulds/rings can be homemade using piping obtained from hardware stores. Cut to required lengths and wash well.

Preheat the oven to 200°C/400°F/Gas Mark 6.

Roll the pastry thinly and rest in the refrigerator for 10 minutes. Cut 8 discs, using the rings to set the 'pies' in. Bake the discs on greaseproof paper for 10–15 minutes. To keep them absolutely flat, another sheet of

Serves 6–8

For the pastry
125 g sweet shortcrust pastry (add a pinch of cinnamon to the flour, if you like) (see page 180)

For the apples
8 x 5 cm x 2.5 cm rings

8 Granny Smith apples, peeled and cored
knob of butter
1 tablespoon light soft brown sugar
apple purée (see page 97) *or* 1 jar apple purée (optional)

paper and a baking tray can be placed on top during the cooking time. Leave to cool.

Cut the apples into rings 2–3 mm thick. Heat the butter in a frying pan and fry the apples quickly on both sides, a few at a time, until they have coloured and are just beginning to soften. When they are all coloured, add more butter and return all of the apple rings to the pan. Toss them in the butter and sprinkle over the sugar, which will caramelise, giving all of the rings a golden finish. Add a teaspoon or two of water, if necessary, to ensure that the caramel covers all of them. Leave to cool.

Grease the moulds and begin to stack the apple slices. After the first 3 slices, spread half a teaspoon of apple purée on top, then continue to stack, adding purée after every 2 slices. Finish with a touch of purée on the top. The apples will be slightly above each mould. Cover them with cling-film, and sit a weighted tray on top of them. Chill until needed. (If you have used metal rings remove them before microwaving, or bake the apples in the oven for 15 minutes to warm them through.)

To serve, sit the warm apple 'pie' cakes on top of the pastry discs, and remove the moulds/rings. To finish either sprinkle Demerara sugar or dust icing sugar across the top, and glaze, as for a crème brûlée, either under the grill or with a gas gun (see page 11). You now have a shiny, crispy golden topping on the open apple pies. These can now be presented as featured on page xx. Warm Sauce Anglaise (see page 191) can be offered separately or perhaps a small scroll of Apple Ice-cream (see page 98) for the ultimate finish.

Inside and Out Orange Pudding

The 'inside and out' of this recipe is all to do with the marmalade, which is incorporated in the sponge itself and also makes the glaze. It is a moist, soft, rich pudding, simple to make and heaven to eat.

Preheat the oven to 190°C/375°F/Gas Mark 5.

Cream together the butter and caster sugar with the orange zest. Stir in the egg yolks, then the self-raising flour. Now add the marmalade, the orange juice and the milk. Whisk the egg whites to soft peaks and gently fold into the pudding mix. Spoon into the dish and put it in a roasting tray. Pour hot water into the tray approximately 1 cm deep. Bake for 50–55 minutes until it is golden brown.

To glaze, mix the marmalade with 3–4 teaspoons of water and warm together. Brush the glaze over the sponge and serve. It goes well with either Orange or plain Sauce Anglaise (see page 191).

Note: For a St Clements Pudding, glaze with lemon marmalade. Or try it with just about any other flavoured marmalade or jam.

Serves 4

1 x 900 ml–1.2 l pudding dish, buttered

50 g butter
100 g caster sugar
grated zest of 1 orange
2 eggs, separated
75 g self-raising flour
3 tablespoons marmalade, coarse *or* fine
juice from 2 oranges, boiled and reduced by two-thirds and cooled
600 ml milk
2 tablespoons fine-cut *or* shredless marmalade for glazing

Apple and Almond Bake

This can be made into one large pudding but I prefer to use individual size 1 soufflé dishes, which are bigger than size 1 ramekins.

The pudding has an apple purée base (you could buy this ready-made) topped with the almond cake and apple wedges fried in butter on top. Apples and almonds have always been good friends, and this dessert combines different textures too, from chunky to smooth.

Make the purée. Stew the apples in a saucepan with the sugar and lemon juice until completely tender. Now purée them in a blender or food-processor. Check the flavour for sweetness, and add more sugar if necessary. Leave to cool.

The almond cake mix: cream together the butter and sugar, then beat in the egg. Now fold in the ground almonds.

Now for the fried apples: melt the butter in a frying pan and put in the apples. After a minute or two add the sugar. This will begin to caramelise, which will help to colour the apples to a golden brown. Once tender, remove the apples from the pan and leave to cool.

Preheat the oven to 180°C/350°F/Gas Mark 4.

To assemble the pudding, divide the purée between the soufflé dishes. Spoon the almond cake mix on top to 5 mm below the rim of the dishes. Arrange 4 or 5 pieces of apple on top of each dish and bake for 20–25 minutes. The almond cake will have risen, but still have kept a moist texture.

The puddings will have a good golden finish, but if you'd prefer something even richer, then either dust them with caster or Demerara sugar, or brush with golden syrup, and caramelise under the grill. All you need now is the custard!

Note: The grated zest of a lemon can be added to the cake mix for extra flavour. Or try a pinch of cinnamon in either the cake mix or the apple purée for Apple and Cinnamon Almond Bake. If using one large dish/basin, the cooking time will be 35–40 minutes.

Serves 4

4 x size 1 soufflé dishes *or* 1 large pudding dish/basin, buttered

For the apple purée
3–4 Bramley cooking apples, peeled, cored and roughly chopped
3 tablespoons caster sugar
squeeze of lemon juice

For the almond cake
100 g unsalted butter
100 g caster sugar
1 egg, beaten
100 g ground almonds

For the fried apple pieces
2 Granny Smith apples, peeled, cored and each cut into 8–10 wedges
25 g unsalted butter
1 teaspoon caster sugar

1 quantity Sauce Anglaise (see page 191)

Baked Plum, Almond and Lemon Pizza

Serves 8

For the 'parmesan'
zest of 4 lemons, finely grated
caster sugar, to bind

For the base
1 x 25–30 cm pizza base,
    greased
1 quantity sweet shortcrust
    pastry (see page 180)

For the frangipane filling
100 g unsalted butter
100 g caster sugar
2 eggs
75 g ground almonds
zest and juice of 2 lemons (juice
    boiled and reduced by half)
25 g plain flour

For the plums
knob of butter
8–10 plums, halved and stoned
1–2 tablespoons soft light brown
    sugar
few tablespoons water

Note: The lemon 'parmesan' is
great to offer with so many other
desserts – most ice-creams, for
example.

It's great fun having a dinner party, or any party for that matter, and telling your friends that it's pizza for pudding! But just imagine the reaction when they see the luscious caramelised plums sitting in the lemon-scented golden frangipane … And it's even finished with 'Parmesan'. For perfect 'Parmesan' make 24 hours in advance.

Work enough caster sugar into the lemon zest to create granules. Spread this in a tray and leave in a warm place for 24 hours. It will form crunchy lemon bittersweet granules. The drying time can be shortened by placing the tray into a very low oven for a few hours but it's important not to colour the granules: you will lose the bright yellow colour.

Preheat the oven to 200°C/400°F/Gas Mark 6.

Line the tin with the pastry and rest it in the fridge. Then line the pastry with greaseproof paper and baking beans or rice. Bake for 15–20 minutes. Remove from the oven and allow to cool. Do not switch off the oven.

For the filling, cream together the butter and caster sugar. Beat in one egg at a time, sprinkling in a little ground almond with each egg to help cream the mix. Add the grated lemon zest and then fold in the remaining ground almonds and flour. Lastly, stir in the lemon juice. Spread the filling in the cooled pastry case, filling it three-quarters full.

Now heat the butter in a large frying pan. Once bubbling, put in the plums, flesh side down. Increase the heat and pan-fry to give golden, almost burnt, edges. Add a tablespoon or two of the soft brown sugar, which will caramelise the plums. (They do not have to cook completely: they will finish off when you bake the pizza.) Add a little water to the pan, to make a caramel syrup that will coat the plums. Remove the pan from the heat, put the plums on a plate to cool, and keep the syrup to glaze the finished dish.

Lay the cooled plums, skin side down, on the almond and lemon filling. Bake for 20–25 minutes until golden. The maximum cooking time should be no more than 30 minutes. Remove from the oven, lift out of the tin, on the loose base, and brush the pizza with the syrup. Sprinkle over the 'parmesan'. Present the pizza on any extra-large plate.

Apple and Blackberry Pudding with Lemon and Golden Syrup

Blackberries are one of my favourite 'summer fruits', with so much taste and texture to offer. When I think of Apple and Blackberry 'Anything' my mouth just starts to water. You can make this recipe just using blackberries and offer apple ice-cream (see page 98) to go with it for a totally different pudding with the same ingredients.

Preheat the oven to 180°C/350°F/Gas Mark 4.

Halve each apple quarter, so that you have 8 pieces from each apple. Using a trickle of the melted butter, lightly pan-fry the apples with the caster sugar for 2–3 minutes, until they have a slightly softer texture, then remove them from the heat, drain off any excess butter, add the lemon juice and allow the apples to cool. Then mix them with the blackberries and put them in the ovenproof dish. Beat the eggs with the soft brown sugar and golden syrup. Stir in the remaining butter, zest and the milk. Sift the self-raising flour with the cinnamon and mix it into the eggs. Pour the batter over the apples and blackberries and bake for 30–35 minutes until the topping is golden and just firm. The pudding is at its best served warm to hot with Sauce Anglaise (see page 191), cream or crème fraîche. The slightly sour flavour of crème fraîche gives a good balance with the sweet filling.

Note: Frozen apples and blackberries or tinned fillings/fruits can be used in this recipe.

Serves 6–8

1 x 20–25 cm shallow ovenproof dish, buttered

4 green dessert apples, peeled, cored and quartered
50 g caster sugar
100 g melted butter
zest and juice of 1 lemon
450 g blackberries
2 eggs
50 g soft brown sugar
2 large tablespoons golden syrup
120 ml milk
225 g self-raising flour
1 heaped teaspoon ground cinnamon

Baked and Sliced Roly Poly

Serves 4–6

1 x 1.2 l ovenproof pudding
   baking dish, buttered

For the syrup
zest and juice of 1 lemon
1 tablespoon golden syrup
50 g light soft brown sugar
15 g butter
125 ml water

450 g fresh fruit – peaches,
   plums, apricots, apples –
   prepared and roughly chopped

225 g self-raising flour, sifted
pinch of salt
100 g suet
water, approximately 150 ml to
   mix
1 tablespoon light soft brown
   sugar
fruit jam (optional)

Jam Roly Poly is another of our great British puddings, but this one is a little different, filled with juicy chopped fruit – plums, peaches, apples, apricots ... the choice is yours.

To make the syrup, heat all of the ingredients together until simmering. Cook for a few minutes and then leave to stand.

Preheat the oven to 190°C/375°F/Gas Mark 5.

To make the suet dough, mix the flour and salt with the suet. Add the water to make a pliable dough. Roll it out on a floured surface to a 25 cm square, about 5 mm thick. Spread with the flavoured jam, if using, then sprinkle over the fruit and roll into a cylinder. Cut it into 2.5 cm thick slices and lay them flat in the baking dish. Strain the syrup and pour it over the roly-poly slices. Bake for 30–40 minutes until the pudding is puffed and golden brown.

To serve, dust the sliced roly-poly with icing sugar. It goes beautifully with Sauce Anglaise (page 191).

Note: Vanilla ice-cream is great with this dish. You can also use tinned fruit or pureé instead of fresh. Instead of baking it, you could wrap it in loose greaseproof paper and steam it for 50–60 minutes, until it is risen and firm to the touch.

Pear and Cinnamon Bake

Serves 4

1 x 900 ml–1.2 l oven proof
   pudding basin, buttered

2 large pears, peeled, cored and
   quartered
150 g butter, plus a knob for
   frying the pears
90 g Demerara sugar
2 tablespoons golden syrup
120 g caster sugar
2 eggs, beaten
150 g self-raising flour, sifted
½ teaspoon ground cinnamon
2 tablespoons milk

This is an upside down pudding with pears bubbling in a treacle base and cinnamon sponge baking on top. When it's turned out the treacle on the pears trickles stickily down and around the sponge. Why not try it with apples instead of the pears?

Preheat the oven to 200°C/400°F/Gas Mark 6.

Cut the 8 pear quarters in half, so that you have 16 slices. Heat the knob of butter in a frying pan and fry the pears gently until just becoming tender. Leave to cool.

Melt 25 g of the butter with the Demerara sugar and the golden syrup and stir them together until the sugar has dissolved. Pour the syrup into the greased pudding basin or dish. Lay the pears on top. Cream together the remaining butter and the caster sugar. Slowly beat in the eggs, then fold in the flour and the cinnamon. Add the milk to soften.

Spoon the pudding mix on top of the pears and bake for approximately 1 hour, until firm to the touch and golden. Turn out the pudding on to a plate to reveal the rich pear topping.

Note: Add the grated zest of a lemon to the sponge mix for a zingy finish. The cinnamon can be omitted altogether or replaced with mixed spice.

Apricot Charlotte Chantilly

A great chance to use up some stale bread! In this Charlotte it becomes crisp and golden on the outside but stays soft and moist inside where it absorbs the fragrant juices of the apricots. You don't have to use apricots – pears, peaches, plums will work just as well. Hot Apple Charlotte is the classic version, but I felt we'd got enough apples in this book – time for them to move over and make room for friends!

Serves 4

4 x 8 cm wide x 5 cm deep metal
  pudding/dariole moulds *or* 1 x
  900 ml–1.2 l metal bowl *or* 1 x
  12.5–15 cm round cake tin

450 g stale bread
butter, for spreading and for
  cooking the apricots
750–900 g apricots, halved,
  stones removed
50 g caster sugar
2 tablespoons apricot jam
1 x Chantilly Cream (see page 185)

Preheat oven to 220°C/425°F/Gas Mark 7.

Cut 4 bread discs to fit the bases of the moulds, and 4 to fit the tops. (If you are using a large bowl, make one of each.) Cut the crusts off the remaining bread and cut it into 3 cm fingers. Butter all of the bread on one side only. Place the smaller discs, butter side down, in the base of the mould. The fingers can now be laid, butter side against the mould, overlapping all the way round.

Cut the apricots into rough 1 cm dice. Melt a knob of butter in a large saucepan and, once bubbling, add the apricots. Turn them for 1–2 minutes, then add the sugar, and continue to turn them. After a minute, remove the pan from the heat. The apricots will not be completely cooked. Add the apricot jam and stir it in. Taste for sweetness, and if necessary add more sugar or jam. Divide the apricots between the Charlottes, then top with the lids. Any excess bread at the sides should be folded over the tops to keep the lids in place. Cook for 30–35 minutes, or 50–60 minutes for a large one, until golden and crispy. Turn out the Charlottes on to plates, and serve with a good spoonful of Chantilly Cream (see page 185). Fresh custard or ice-cream go well with this dish.

Calvados Apple Cobbler

A cobbler is a traditional British pudding that contains similar ingredients to a crumble. The difference is that the crumble topping here is turned into scones, which rise to a good crusty topping while the underneath stays moist with the juice from the fruit. The Calvados lifts the apple filling to new heights. You can use cider in place of the Calvados: double the quantity, boil it and reduce by half for a stronger flavour.

Melt the butter in a large saucepan, put in the apples and cook for 1–2 minutes. Then add the sugar. Continue to cook for another minute until the sugar has dissolved. Add the raisins, the Calvados, and the cinnamon, if using, and stir all the ingredients together carefully. Check the mix for sweetness: if it is too tart, add the remaining 25 g of sugar. Spoon it into the pudding basin and leave to cool.

Now make the cobbler topping. Preheat the oven to 200°C/400°F/Gas Mark 6. Sift together the flour and salt. Rub in the butter to a crumble consistency. Stir in the sugar along with the grated lemon zest. Add the egg and 2–3 tablespoons of milk and work to a pliable dough. Roll it out on a floured surface until 1 cm thick, and cut it into rounds, 3–5 cm in diameter. Sit the scones on top of the apples, brush with milk and sprinkle with granulated sugar, if using. Bake for 15 minutes, then reduce the oven temperature to 180°C/350°F/Gas Mark 4 and continue to bake for a further 20–25 minutes.

Extra thick cream or Calvados flavoured Sauce Anglaise (see page 191) are perfect with this dish.

Note: The cobbler topping eats very well as tea-time scones!

Serves 4–6

1 x 1.2 l ovenproof pudding dish, buttered

For the apples
knob of butter
900 g cooking apples, peeled, cored and cut into chunks
50–75 g light soft brown sugar
50 g raisins or dates (chopped) (optional)
2–3 measures Calvados
pinch of cinnamon (optional)

For the scone cobbler
225 g self-raising flour
pinch of salt
100 g butter, diced
50 g caster sugar
grated zest of 1 lemon
1 egg
4 tablespoons of milk, plus a little extra
granulated sugar for sprinkling (optional)

Bread and Butter Pudding

Serves 6–8

1 x 1.5–1.8 l pudding dish/basin, buttered

12 medium slices white bread, crusts cut off

50 g unsalted butter, softened

1 vanilla pod *or* a few drops of vanilla essence

300 ml double cream

300 ml milk

8 egg yolks

175 g caster sugar, plus extra for the caramelised topping

25 g sultanas

25 g raisins

In my first cookery book, I said that this recipe has become one of our (my) great classics. What an understatement! For me, it is probably our greatest classic and stands for everything that Sweet Dreams is about. At one time Bread and Butter Pudding provided an excuse to use up old bread, which was sprinkled with a few raisins and sultanas, then baked, with some eggs, milk and sugar, until the fruit on top resembled the after-effects of a rabbit's visit!

So how has it changed? The fruit on top has disappeared, for a start and the custard is rich – only egg yolks are used. It is absorbed by the bread, which sort of soufflés and becomes almost a soft sponge. The crispy topping is slightly bitter, but that helps to balance the sweet, thick, spongy custard. Once you cut it, the custard just starts to dribble on to the plate, telling you that it's been worth every minute and every penny you've spent in making it.

The ingredients look extravagant but if you want to go even further use 450 ml of double cream to 150 ml of milk …

Preheat the oven to 180°C/350°F/Gas Mark 4.

Butter the bread. Split the vanilla pod and place in a saucepan with the cream and milk and bring to the boil. While it is heating, whisk together the egg yolks and caster sugar in a bowl. Allow the cream mix to cool a little, then strain it on to the egg yolks, stirring all the time. You now have the custard.

Cut the bread into triangular quarters or halves, and arrange in the dish in three layers, sprinkling the fruit between two layers and leaving the top clear. Now pour over the warm custard, lightly pressing the bread to help it soak in, and leave it to stand for at least 20–30 minutes before cooking to ensure that the bread absorbs all the custard.

The pudding can be prepared to this stage several hours in advance and cooked when needed. Place the dish in a roasting tray three-quarters filled with warm water and

bake for 20–30 minutes until the pudding begins to set. Don't overcook it or the custard will scramble. Remove the pudding from the water bath, sprinkle it liberally with caster sugar and glaze under the grill on a medium heat or with a gas gun (see page 11) to a crunchy golden finish. When glazing, the sugar dissolves and caramelises, and you may find that the corners of the bread begin to burn. This helps the flavour, giving a bittersweet taste that mellows when it is eaten with the rich custard, which seeps out of the wonderful bread sponge when you cut into it. Sweet Dreams come true!

Roast Sticky Fruits

Serves 2

75 g butter
1 peach, stoned and quartered
1 plum, stoned and halved (2 for
   larger portion)
1 apricot, stoned and halved (2
   for larger portion)
1 thick (2.5 cm) round slice of
   pineapple, quartered
1 fig, stoned and quartered
1 banana (*or* 2 finger bananas),
   quartered
4–6 strawberries
2 tablespoons light soft brown
   sugar
2–3 tablespoons water
2 measures brandy
extra thick cream or vanilla ice-
   cream to serve with the dish

When just the two of you are eating and you're stuck for a pudding, it's time to raid the fruit basket. What you use is up to you (or the basket!). I've listed several different ones here – they all love the sticky, boozy finish. And so will you!

Heat half of the butter in a large frying pan. Once bubbling, put in the pieces of peach, plum, apricot and pineapple. Cook on a medium heat for a few minutes, then turn the fruit over. Add the fig, strawberries and bananas and increase the heat, allowing all to colour. After a few minutes the fruit should all be tender. Sprinkle with the sugar, which will start to caramelise in the pan and on the fruit. Turn the fruit over and add the water. This will dissolve any sugar crystals and make an instant syrup. Stir gently and, holding the edge of the pan near the open flame, add the brandy and flambé (if using an electric cooker, set it alight with a long match or lighter). Shake the pan gently and present to your guest while still flaming. Divide the fruit on to the plates with the sticky sweet brandy syrup poured over. Offer extra thick cream or ice-cream to go with it.

Note: The fruit can be fried to colour quickly on both sides, then cooked in a preheated oven (200°C/400°F/Gas Mark 6) for approximately 6–8 minutes until tender. Take out the pan, bring it back to the stove and heat before adding the sugar and water, and finishing with the brandy.

Peach Clafoutis

Clafoutis is a famous French dessert from Provence. The name has come from the Provençal dialect word clafir, *to fill. Batter is baked with fresh fruit, either poached, roasted or raw, to a golden brown and finished with a dusting of icing sugar. Originally sour black cherries were used but you can put in whatever you like! Good quality tinned fruit will do instead of fresh. This dessert is very moreish. The clafoutis featured here have been made in 18 cm x 5 cm 'sur le plat' dishes. For smaller portions 12.5 cm x 10 cm dishes can be used.*

Preheat the oven to 180°C/350°F/Gas Mark 4.

First cook the peaches. Melt the butter in a frying pan and put them in, cut side down. Cook on a medium heat for 1 minute, then sprinkle in the sugar. Continue to cook until the peaches have a caramel-golden finish. Turn them over, remove the pan from the stove and let them cool. Arrange them in the baking dish.

Make the batter. Bring the milk to the boil with the vanilla pod. Remove from the heat and allow to infuse for 5–6 minutes. Add the whipping cream and Amaretto, if using, to the milk and strain through a sieve. Whisk the eggs, the sugar and the salt until it forms thick creamy ribbons. Fold the egg mix into the cream. Sift the flour into the batter, stir it in and pour it over the peaches.

Bake for 25–30 minutes, until it is set and golden brown. Dust with icing sugar and serve *immediately*. A good spoonful of extra thick cream goes very well with the clafoutis.

Note: The flour can be replaced with ground almonds to intensify the flavour of the Amaretto. The 'sur le plat' 18 cm dish is coded D36 1; the 12.5 cm dish is D 36 0. The coding is found on the base of the dish.

Serves 2–4

1 x large baking dish, buttered,
   or 2 x 'sur le plat' dishes,
   pictured above

For the peaches
50 g butter
6 small peaches, halved, stones
   removed
50 g caster sugar

For the batter
50 ml milk
1 vanilla pod, split *or* few drops
   of essence
75 ml whipping cream
25 ml Amaretto (optional)
2 eggs
175 g caster sugar
15 g flour
pinch of salt

Upside Down Fig Pudding

Serves 6

6 x 7.5 cm x 6 cm rings *or* 6 x
   150 ml pudding basins *or* 1 x
   900 ml–1.2 l pudding basin *or*
   flan ring, greased

6 fresh figs
125 g butter
125 g caster sugar
4 whole eggs
1 egg yolk
80 g ground almonds
80 g plain flour

For the coulis
60 g caster sugar
120–150 ml water
1–2 tablespoons port

I feel that figs are a fruit that none of us uses often enough. Hopefully this recipe will inspire you to try them. Not only is the pudding upside down, but when you eat it your opinion of figs will also be turned ... upside down!

Preheat the oven 180°C/350°F/Gas Mark 4.

Sit the rings, if using, on a greased baking tray.

Cut 3 x 5 mm thick slices from each fig, saving all trimmings for a fig coulis. To make the coulis, chop the fig trimmings and place them in a small saucepan with the water and the caster sugar. Bring to a simmer and cook until the figs are completely tender.

Liquidise to a purée and push through a sieve. If it seems too thin, put it in a saucepan and boil it until it has reduced to a thicker consistency. For more body and a better finish, stir in the port.

To make the puddings, cream together the butter and caster sugar. Lightly fork the eggs with the egg yolk and beat slowly into the butter mix. Fold in the flour and ground almonds. If you are using individual moulds, place a slice of fig in the base of each. Spoon or pipe (piping is a lot easier) some of the pudding mix on top. Sit another slice of fig on top and repeat the same process until you have used 3 slices of fig per mould, finishing with sponge on top.

If you are using one large mould make a circular pattern of fig slices on the base, and continue as for the smaller moulds. Bake the pudding(s): 20–25 minutes for individual ones, and 40–50 minutes for a large one.

Remove from the oven and turn the pudding(s) out of the mould(s), to reveal a wonderful golden sponge with a slice of fig showing through the top. Dribble over and around with the fig and port coulis. You can serve the Upside Down Fig Pudding with either pouring cream, thick cream, clotted cream or Sauce Anglaise (see page 191) – along with the Port and Lemon Sorbet (page 91) – I think that's enough to choose from for now!

Glazed Amarula Custard Creams

Serves 6

6 x size 1 ramekins

150 ml milk
450 ml double cream
8 egg yolks
80 g caster sugar
7 tablespoons Amarula

Amarula is a liqueur taken from the fruit of the wild marula tree, which grows in southern Africa and is known locally as the elephant tree, because elephants like to eat its tasty yellow fruits. Amarula has its own distinctive taste – impossible to describe, apart from delicious! Try it simply poured over ice or in your coffee.

Preheat the oven 180°C/350°F/Gas Mark 4.

Bring the milk and cream to the boil. Whisk together the egg yolks and sugar until they are light and pale. Pour the boiled cream on to the yolks and continue to whisk. Stir in the Amarula and divide the mix between the ramekins. Place these in a roasting tray and half fill it with warm water.

Bake the creams until they are just setting. Check after 20 minutes by shaking a ramekin gently: the cream should still have slight movement in the centre but if it is too loose, continue to cook for a further 5–10 minutes. Remove the ramekins from the tray and leave to cool.

Sprinkle sifted icing sugar over the top of each ramekin. Wipe away any excess from the rim and caramelise under a hot grill or with a gas gun (see page 11). Repeat at least once, preferably twice, to give a thin, crispy glazed topping. The puddings are at their best at room temperature. For a firmer, chilled finish, place in the refrigerator for 1–2 hours.

Note: Thinly sliced bananas can be overlapped on top of the creams before glazing. Substitute one glazing of icing sugar for a sprinkling of Demerara sugar for a crunchy, grainy finish. Bailey's will also work well in this recipe, or you can leave out the liqueur altogether for Crème Brûlée.

Crème Brûlée

No-one can ever agree on whether this dish is classic French or British but it's so good to eat that I love to claim it's British. Somehow, though, the name Burnt Cream doesn't hold the same melting experience as Crème Brûlée! Anyway, this dish is just too good to be ignored, wherever it came from!

It can be served cold (refrigerated) or at room temperature but I really do believe that the best way to eat Crème Brûlée is at room temperature. The custard is just at setting point and holds its full vanilla flavour. If refrigerated I find it becomes overchilled and doesn't release its full flavour – the texture may even become 'cakey'. Anyway, the choice is yours. The one advantage of eating it cold is knowing that it has definitely set!

Preheat the oven to 180°C/350°F/Gas Mark 4.

Mix together the egg yolks and sugar in a bowl. Bring the cream to the boil with the vanilla pod or essence. Remove the pod and scrape the seeds into the cream. Now whisk the cream into the egg yolks and sugar. Sit the bowl over a pan of lightly simmering water and heat until the custard begins to thicken, stirring all the time. It should have the consistency of single cream.

Now divide the custard between the ramekins. Put these in a roasting tin and pour in some warm water until it comes three-quarters of the way up the sides of the moulds. Put it into the oven and leave until the Crème Brûlées are just on the point of setting, approximately 20–30 minutes. To test, remove one of the moulds from the water and shake it gently. There should still be a slight movement in the centre of the custard. If it seems a little too runny, return to the oven and check after another 5–10 minutes. Remove from the oven and the roasting tray and allow to cool.

Dust the Brûlées generously with icing sugar, wiping around the edge before you glaze them, either under a preheated grill or with a gas gun (see page 11). As the sugar heats, it begins to dissolve, bubble and to colour: this is the time to redust and rebubble. To achieve a good, rich, crisp topping repeat three times.

Serves 6

6 x size 1 ramekins

8 egg yolks
50 g caster sugar
600 ml double cream
1 vanilla pod, split, *or* a few
  drops of vanilla essence
icing sugar to finish

Burnt Coconut Creams

Serves 6

6 x size 1 ramekins

3 egg yolks
400 ml condensed milk
400 ml milk
200 g fresh finely grated coconut
  or desiccated
icing sugar for glazing

A quick coconut version of Crème Brûlée.

Preheat the oven to 230°C/450°F/Gas Mark 8.

Whisk together the egg yolks and condensed milk, then add the milk and grated coconut. Pour into the ramekins, making sure that the coconut is evenly distributed. Place the ramekins in a roasting tray half filled with warm water. Bake for 12–15 minutes. Remove from the oven and the roasting tray and leave to cool. Dust the coconut creams generously with icing sugar, wipe any excess from the ramekin rims and glaze under the grill or with a gas gun (see page 11). Repeat at least once, preferably twice, for a crisp caramel topping.

Note: Lay thin slices of fresh or tinned pineapple on top of the coconut creams before dusting and glazing, as featured below.

Glazed Lemon Tart

This has become one of the great modern classics, and was introduced to us all by the Roux brothers. I promise you it's a dream: the flavour and texture just stand on their own. You could accompany it with other fruits, such as raspberries, cherries or strawberries, but I like to serve it with just a trickle of cream.

Preheat the oven to 180°C/350°F/Gas Mark 4.

When you are making the pastry add the grated lemon zest to the flour and sugar. Chill the pastry for 20–30 minutes before rolling it and lining the flan ring. Leave to rest on a baking sheet before lining it with greaseproof paper and baking beans, then baking blind for 15–20 minutes. Remove the paper and beans and leave to cool. Reduce the oven temperature to 150°C/300°F/Gas Mark 2.

To make the filling, beat the eggs and caster sugar together until smooth. Add the cream, lemon juice and zest. Pour into the cooked flan ring and bake for 45–50 minutes until the tart is just set. Remove from the oven and allow to cool.

The tart is now ready to serve, but I prefer to glaze it with icing sugar. This will give you a thin crispy topping. Sprinkle the tart with icing sugar and colour under the grill or with a gas gun (see page 11). Repeat for an even crispier finish.

A classic is born!

Serves 8

1 x 20–25 cm x 2.5 cm deep flan ring

½ quantity sweet shortcrust pastry (page 180)
finely grated zest of 1 lemon

For the filling
4 whole eggs
175 g caster sugar
150 ml double cream
2 lemons, juice from all, finely grated zest from 1

For the topping
icing sugar

Crispy Apple Tart

Serves 4

2 large baking trays, buttered

½ quantity puff pastry (page
    181–2) or 225 g bought puff
    pastry
50 g butter
8 Granny Smith apples, peeled,
    cored and quartered
4 teaspoons caster sugar
4 tablespoons apricot jam
2 tablespoons water

For the apple sorbet (optional)
6 Granny Smith apples, peeled,
    cored and roughly chopped
300 ml sweet cider
50–100 g caster sugar

Note: Add a measure or two of
Calvados to the sorbet mix, or a
few drops of lemon juice, for a
richer flavour. If you haven't got
an ice-cream machine, pour the
sorbet mix into a bowl and freeze
until almost completely set. Tip
into a food-processor and blitz to

Many years ago I was working in France at a restaurant called La Lameloise which has three Michelin stars and is where I found this recipe. It was their most popular dessert, and when you've tried it you'll know why!

These tarts can be made to any size you wish but I like to roll out the puff pastry very thinly and cut it into 20 cm discs – that's one per portion! It sounds an awful lot, but it is so thin and crisp that you can fold it into quarters and eat it in three or four bites! 15 cm discs work well too. The tarts are lovely served with a spoonful or two of apple sorbet, so why not try the recipe I've included here?

Preheat the oven to 230°C/450°F/Gas Mark 8.

Roll out the pastry as thinly as possible and leave it to rest. Cut it into 4 x 20 cm discs. If you find only 3 can be cut, then re-roll the pastry trimmings to make the fourth.

Lay the tart bases on the baking trays and leave to rest in the fridge. Cut each apple quarter into 4–5 slices, and arrange them on top of the pastry discs, starting at the outside and overlapping the slices all the way round. Then start again towards the middle, again overlapping. To finish sit 2–3 slices in the centre.

Chop the butter and dot it over the tarts. Sprinkle each with caster sugar and bake for 15–20 minutes until the pastry is crisp and the apples have started to colour.

Boil the apricot jam with the water and brush each tart to give a rich glazed finish. They are now ready to serve.

To make the sorbet, mix all the ingredients together, adding just 50 g of the caster sugar. Bring to a simmer and cook until the apples are tender. Drain off the cooking liquor and reduce it by half. This will increase the flavour and sweetness. Now add the apples to the liquor and blitz the whole lot in a blender or food-processor to a purée. Taste for sweetness: if it is too tart, bring it to a simmer with more caster sugar. Leave to cool, then churn in an ice-cream machine until thick and almost frozen. Allow to set completely in the freezer.

Treacle Tart

Serves 6

1 x 18 cm x 2.5 cm flan ring,
  buttered

200 g sweet shortcrust pastry
  (see page 180)

For the filling
250 g golden syrup
zest and juice of 1 lemon
250 g fresh white breadcrumbs,
  about 8 slices from a medium
  white loaf with crusts removed
25 ml double cream
1 egg yolk

This is a pudding I often feature as part of the British Pudding Plate. It's so moist and moreish and has to be one of the easiest tarts to make.

Preheat the oven to 200°C/400°F/Gas Mark 6.

Line the flan ring with the pastry, then with greaseproof paper and baking beans. Bake for 15 minutes until just golden. Do not switch off the oven.

For the filling, warm the syrup, lemon juice and zest together. Stir in the breadcrumbs and add the cream. Pour it into the pastry case and bake for approximately 20 minutes until it is light golden. Leave it to cool before removing it from the flan ring. Treacle Tart is best served at room temperature, with extra thick cream.

Gypsy Tart

I had been searching for this recipe for years – it was one of the few school-dinner puddings I ever looked forward to! When eventually I got hold of the recipe I just couldn't believe how simple it was. The filling, as you can see, has just two ingredients, held together with the pastry case.

Some time ago I featured this recipe in one of my television programmes and many people wrote to me, telling me how much they enjoyed it. However, many others wrote saying that the recipe just did not work! I can only promise you that this recipe is foolproof!

Preheat the oven to 200°C/400°F/Gas Mark 6.

Roll out the pastry and use it to line the flan ring. Line the pastry with greaseproof paper and baking beans, and bake blind for 15–20 minutes. Remove the beans and paper and leave to cool. If you haven't had time to refrigerate the evaporated milk, it will still work but when you whisk it with the sugar it takes longer to achieve the correct consistency. Now, using an electric mixer or food-processor, whisk together the evaporated milk and sugar, on full power for a minimum 12–15 minutes. By this time it will have become light, coffee-coloured and creamy. The consistency should resemble softly whipped cream that's not quite holding peaks.

Now pour it into the pastry case and bake for 10 minutes, during which the filling will 'set', with a sticky surface. Remove it from the oven and leave to cool. Once at room temperature, the Gypsy Tart is ready to cut and serve. It really is a very easy recipe but gives great results. I like to serve it with pouring cream.

Note: The Gypsy Tart is always best served at room temperature. If you refrigerate it for several hours or overnight, you will find that the sugar turns into a dark syrup and begins to leak out of the tart. So what I'm saying is this – cook it and eat it!

Serves 8–12

1 x 25 cm flan ring, buttered

½ quantity shortcrust pastry (see page 180)
1 x 400 g tin evaporated milk, refrigerated
275 g Tate & Lyle dark soft brown cane sugar

Open Caramelised Pineapple Tartlet

Serves 6

1 baking tray, lined with greased
   parchment paper, 10 cm
   shallow tin tartlet case(s) and
   1 x 11–12 cm plastic stencil (see
   page 178)
1 x 28 cm x 18 cm Swiss roll tin,
   greased

For the coconut tartlet cases
30 g butter
40 g light soft brown sugar
45 g liquid glucose
40 g plain flour
30 g desiccated coconut

For the coffee cake
1 tablespoon instant coffee
1 teaspoon hot water
100 g self-raising flour
1 teaspoon baking powder
100 g butter
100 g caster sugar
2 eggs
75 g chopped walnuts (optional)

This recipe contains four components but don't feel obliged to make them all: the caramelised pineapple is great on its own with pouring cream, a bought ice-cream or the coconut ice-cream. The pineapples can also be made well in advance and reheated before serving.

Preheat the oven to 180°C/350°F/Gas Mark 4.

Make the coconut tartlet cases first. Cream together the butter, sugar and glucose. Add the flour and coconut and mix well. Spread the mix, using the stencil, on the lined baking tray. Bake for 6–8 minutes. Remove the tray from the oven and shape the discs in the tartlet case(s) (if unavailable, use a bowl or saucer). If the biscuits become too hard to shape, soften them in the warm oven before continuing. Keep them in an air-tight container until you need them.

To make the cake, preheat the oven to 170°C/325°F/Gas Mark 3. Dissolve the coffee in the hot water. Now mix together all the ingredients until totally combined and spread in the Swiss roll tin. Bake for 20 minutes until just firm to the touch. Remove from the oven and allow to cool. Turn the sponge out from the tin and cut discs to fit the tartlets.

To make the ice-cream, pour the milk, cream and coconut milk into a saucepan along with the desiccated coconut and bring it to the boil. While it is heating, whisk the egg yolks and sugar together. When the cream boils, pour it over the egg mix, whisking as you go. Put the bowl over a pan of water and cook gently on a moderate heat (do not boil or the eggs will scramble) until it coats the back of a spoon. Now leave it to cool before churning for 20–25 minutes, or until thick and creamy, in an ice-cream machine. Put it in the freezer to finish setting. (If you haven't got an ice-cream machine, see page 83.)

Split the pineapple through the centre lengthways, then again to give you four quarters. Remove the central core and cut into 16–24 wedges. Heat the butter in a large frying pan. Once it is bubbling, put in the pineapple pieces, 6–8 pieces at a time, and cook for a few minutes on each side. Increase the heat and add the caster sugar. This will immediately begin to caramelise. As it turns golden turn the pineapple to spread the flavour. Add the water –

For the coconut ice-cream
250 ml milk
280 ml double or whipping
   cream
100 ml coconut milk
50 g desiccated coconut
6 egg yolks
100 g caster sugar

For the caramelised pineapple
1 large pineapple, skinned
large knob of butter
2–3 tablespoons caster sugar
2–3 tablespoons water
icing sugar, to finish

it will lift the caramelised sugar from the base of the pan and make a thick caramel to coat the pineapple. Repeat until you have cooked all the pineapple. Set it to one side. Pour a little warm water into the pan to release any remaining caramel, for dribbling over the finished dish.

To assemble the dish, dust the plates or bowls with icing sugar through a tea-strainer. This is not essential, but makes a good effect. Put a tartlet case on each plate, and sit in it a coffee sponge disc. Reheat the pineapple wedges and arrange on top of the sponges. Dribble over any excess syrup. You can serve the coconut ice-cream as an accompaniment or scooped on top of each tart.

Note: Once the ice-cream mix has cooled and thickened it can be passed through a sieve to remove the desiccated coconut. For a quicker ice-cream (if an ice-cream machine is unavailable), warm the coconut milk with the desiccated coconut. Leave to cool. Then mix it with half a 425 g tin or carton of ready-made custard and 150 ml of lightly whipped cream. Freeze and your ice-cream is ready. You can add 2–3 tablespoons (or more!) of Malibu for an even more intense flavour.

Chocolate Tart

The title of this dish sounds pretty plain – just Chocolate Tart – but I quite enjoy giving dishes very simple titles and the real secret lies in the dish itself. Chocolate seems to be showing its face quite a bit in this book – but why not? There are so many different textures and tastes being achieved with it, and a good chocolate dessert helps many sweet dreams!

Preheat the oven to 200°C/400°F/Gas Mark 6.

First line the tart case with the pastry, then with greaseproof paper and baking beans. Bake for 20–30 minutes until golden and crisp. Remove the paper and beans and leave to cool. Reduce the oven temperature to 100°C/220°F/Gas Mark ¼.

To make the filling, melt the chocolate in a bowl over simmering water. Bring the milk and cream to the boil and while it is heating, lightly beat the eggs. Once the milk is boiling, pour it on to the eggs whisking as you go. Strain the mixture over the melted chocolate and mix well. Pour the filling into the cooked pastry case. Bake for 30 minutes for individual tarts and 45–60 for a large one. The chocolate tarts are best eaten warm or cold, with Sauce Anglaise (see page 191) or the Milk Chocolate and Coffee Custard (see page 191) – pure indulgence!

Note: As an extra garnish I like to top this tart with chocolate shavings (see page 198). Milk chocolate would contrast well with the dark chocolate filling.

Serves 8–10

1 x 25–30 cm flan ring,
  or 8–10 x 10 cm x 5 cm
  individual fluted flan rings,
  greased

1½ quantity sweet shortcrust
  pastry (see page 180)

500 g plain dark chocolate,
  chopped
200 ml milk
350 ml double cream
3 whole eggs

Fruit Tarts

One of the most seductive puddings: juicy fruit sitting on a crispy pastry base with Pastry Cream (see page 184), Crème Chiboust (see page 186), or a simple vanilla Chantilly (see page 185) to enrich the whole experience.

Tarts can take on so many different faces. The pastry cases can be precooked, filled with creams, jams or both, then topped with cooked, tinned or fresh fruit. They can be built and cooked from raw, then brushed with a rich glaze to leave a wonderful shine. They can be made individually, using round or boat-shaped barquette cases. They can be made from a choice of pastries: puff, shortcrust or sweet shortcrust (see pages 180–1) will all give you the crispness you're looking for.

One golden rule: never refrigerate a tart. They should be served just cold or warm. If refrigerated, the pastry becomes soggy and chewy, and the fruit loses its liveliness.

225–275 g puff, shortcrust *or* sweet shortcrust pastry (see pages 180–2)

All of the tarts in this section take a 20–25 cm flan ring *or* 7.5 cm round or boat-shaped cases, lightly greased.

Let's start with the pastry case.

Preheat the oven to 220°C/425°F/Gas Mark 7.

Roll the pastry on a floured surface to approximately 3 mm thick and use it to line the flan ring. Trim off the excess and pinch the edges with your thumb and forefinger for an attractive finish. Or, leave the excess pastry hanging over the edge, crimping it lightly to hold it in place. Once cooked, the edge can be cut level with a sharp knife against the flan ring. This doesn't give you quite such a pretty finish, but guarantees no shrinking of the pastry into the flan ring. Prick the pastry base all over with a fork, then refrigerate and rest it for 20 minutes before baking. When ready to bake, line it with greaseproof paper and baking beans, then bake for 20–25 minutes until golden and crispy. Remove from the oven, and take out the paper and beans. Leave to cool. Small individual cases may take only 15–20 minutes. If you are baking the tart with raw fruit, follow this method to the point at which it is put to rest in the refrigerator.

Now for the fillings!

strawberries; wild strawberries; raspberries; blackberries; red and white currants.

Soft red fruits:

Blind-bake the tart case, allow it to cool, then spread with Pastry Cream, Crème Chiboust or Chantilly (see pages 184, 186 and 185), and lay the fruit on top. Leave either as they are, or dusted with icing sugar, or brushed with a glaze which can be made from either redcurrant jelly or raspberry jam. If you decide to use Pastry Cream pour it still warm into the cooked case and leave it to set. This will give you a good smooth finish, ready to decorate with the fruits.

mango; paw-paw; melon; grapes (black or white); kiwi; banana; pineapple.

Other soft fruits:

All of these can be presented as for the red soft fruits, but make the glaze with apricot jam. For every tablespoon of jam used, add 1–2 tablespoons of water and bring to the boil. Strain it through a tea-strainer or a sieve, then brush over the fruit. If using banana, I like to overlap 5 mm thick slices for a scaled effect. Dust heavily with icing sugar and caramelise under the grill or with a gas gun (see page 11). Cover the edge of the tart case with foil to stop it burning.

rhubarb; gooseberries; damsons; cherries; greengages; apricots; plums.

'Cooking fruits':

All of these fruits can be completely precooked before being put in the pastry cream tart cases, but I feel you get a better result if they are finished off with the pastry. Cherries, however, can be cooked in the pastry from raw. You will need approximately 750 g of cherries. Stone them, keeping them whole, then place them in the raw pastry case, sprinkled with 50–75 g of caster sugar and bake in the preheated oven, 220°C/425°F/Gas Mark 7, for 30–35 minutes. Take out the tart, let it cool and glaze with redcurrant jelly or raspberry jam.

For damsons, plums, greengages and apricots, you will need 750 g. Halve the fruits and remove the stones. Soften the fruit, either by sprinkling it with 50–75 g caster sugar and warming it for 5–10 minutes in the oven or cooking it in a frying pan with a knob of butter and the sugar. (Save any fruit juices released, which can be added to the apricot jam for a stronger-tasting glaze.) Now spread the pastry case with Pastry Cream (the other creams will not work in this cooking method), approximately 6–8 tablespoons. Arrange the fruit on top, packing it in closely, and bake in the preheated oven at 200°C/400°F/Gas Mark 6 for 30–40 minutes. Remove the tart from the oven and leave it to stand for 10–15 minutes before removing the flan ring and allowing it to cool on a wire rack. Then glaze it.

Rhubarb and gooseberries can be cooked directly in the cases on top of the Pastry Cream with 100–175 g of caster sugar to every 750–900 g of fruit. Peel the rhubarb, if stringy, and cut it into 2 cm slices. The gooseberries can be left whole. Roll the fruit in the sugar and pack it into the case. Bake for 35–40 minutes, before resting and glazing. The disadvantage of this method is that the juices from the fruit may prevent the pastry from crisping. Here's an alternative to battle that: spread 6–8 tablespoons of pastry cream in the base of the raw case, then take a 1 cm thick round slice from a 20–25 cm plain or lemon Genoise sponge (see page xx) and lay it on top of the Pastry Cream. Put the fruit on the Genoise, which will absorb the juices, while protecting the pastry case. Bake in a preheated oven at 200°C/400°F/Gas Mark 6. Remove the tart from the oven, allow it to cool a little and then glaze.

Note: Finely grated orange and lemon zest can be added to the Pastry Cream or to the pastry to enhance and give a citrus aroma to the tarts. A twist of black pepper in the pastry livens up the flavour with a hot bite. Peaches, nectarines, blueberries, bilberries, loganberries, tayberries and figs are also scrumptious in tarts! Use your imagination!

Large Eccles Cakes

Serves 4–6

2 apples, peeled and cored

50 g butter, plus a small knob

50 g soft light brown sugar

50 g currants

50 g sultanas

1 dessertspoon mixed candied
peel (optional)

good pinch of cinnamon

zest of 1 lemon, finely grated

250 g quick puff pastry (see
page 182) or bought frozen,
thawed

1 egg white

granulated sugar, for sprinkling

It's not exactly known when Eccles cakes were first made, although we do know that they originated in the Lancashire town of Eccles and have been with us for at least 300 years. Eccles actually means 'church', which derives from the Greek 'ecclesia', meaning 'assembly'. There's an old church in Eccles which was built in 1111. It was here that an annual service, better known as 'Eccles Wakes', took place. After each wake, a local fair was held where food, drink and, in particular, Eccles cake were enjoyed. At one point, in 1650, the wakes and cakes were banned when the Puritans took power – the Eccles for being too rich!

A visitor to the town, Arnold Bennett, the great English novelist, found the bakery where it is claimed that the cakes have been made for hundreds of years. He described the shop as 'the most romantic shop in the world'. With the lightness, crispness and richness this recipe brings, I couldn't agree more.

Preheat the oven to 200°C/400°F/Gas Mark 6.

Cut the apples into rough (2–3 mm) dice. Melt the knob of butter in a saucepan on a medium heat, and add the apples. Cook for a few minutes, until they have just softened. Allow to cool.

Mix the butter with the brown sugar, the fruit, the candied peel, the cinnamon and the lemon zest. Fold in the cooked apples.

Roll the pastry thinly (2–3 mm) into a 30–35 cm disc. Lay it on a baking sheet. Spoon the filling into the centre, approximately 15–18 cm round. Fold in the edges, pressing the pastry lightly together. Rest in the fridge for 15–20 minutes. Take a greased baking sheet and lay it on top of the Eccles cake. Turn it over and you have the presentation side up on the greased tray ready for baking.

Brush the cake with egg white and sprinkle with granulated sugar. Score 6 lines with a sharp knife towards the centre of the cake. Bake for 30–40 minutes until it is crispy and golden. Delicious hot, warm or cold.

Note: If you decide to make individual cakes, cook them for just 25 minutes.

Blueberry and Almond Tart

Apart from the blueberries, this recipe is a collection of several other recipes featured in this book. The finished results are so good, as you can see in the picture, I just had to include it!

Preheat the oven to 180°C/350°F/Gas Mark 4.

Line the tartlet cases with the pastry and trim any excess from the rims. Leave to rest.

Keep back 100 g of the blueberries, and sprinkle half of the rest between all of the cases. Mix the grated lemon zest into the almond frangipane and pipe it or spoon it on top. Scatter the remaining berries over and bake for 15–20 minutes. The tarts will now be just firm to the touch and slightly golden. Remove from the oven and keep warm. Warm the 100 g of blueberries with the icing sugar over a low heat for 5–6 minutes, until tender.

To serve, sit the tartlets in the centre of the plates and spoon the compôte around them. Put a scroll or scoop of the Lemon Curd Ice-cream on top and finish with the Candied Syrup Lemon Strips.

Note: Vanilla or lemon sorbet, homemade or bought, can also be served with this dish. The tartlets can be made well in advance and reheated in a warm oven. Try fresh raspberries, cherries, blackberries or dried chopped apricots in place of the blueberries. A little jam of the fruit you use can be spread into the base of each tartlet case before laying the fruit on top.

Serves 6

6 x 10 cm x 4 cm tartlet cases *or*
   1 x 15–18 cm flan ring

350 g sweet shortcrust pastry
   (see page 180)
200 g almond frangipane (see
   page 28)
zest of 1 lemon, finely grated
275 g blueberries
60 g icing sugar

For the garnish (optional)
1 quantity Lemon Curd Ice-cream
   (see page 86)
Candied Syrup Lemon Strips (see
   page 188)

Rhubarb Fool Tart

Serves 4

For the crispy rhubarb strips
6–8 x 10 cm sticks rhubarb
caster sugar

300 g puff pastry *or* quick puff
    pastry (see pages 181–2) *or*
    frozen puff pastry
1 egg yolk (optional)
a little milk (optional)

For the compôte
400 g fresh rhubarb
100 g caster sugar

For the fool
250 g of the cooked rhubarb
    (above)
150 ml double cream
180 ml Pastry Cream (see page
    184)

This tart is, in fact, a rectangular puff pastry vol-au-vent, filled with a compôte of cooked rhubarb and topped with the fool. It is finished with very thin strips of dried rhubarb, which give you a great visual effect and a complete range of textures from the fruit – crisp, stewed and creamy.

The vol-au-vent cases can be omitted, along with the crispy strips, leaving you with the compôte to present in a glass bowl, topped with the fool. If you want to make the dried strips, start a day ahead.

First make the rhubarb strips: slice the rhubarb lengthways into very thin strips; for consistency, it's best to use a mandolin. Lay the strips on a baking tray lined with parchment paper. Sprinkle lightly with caster sugar and dry out in the oven at its lowest temperature setting for up to 12 hours. Increasing the oven temperature will not dry them any quicker: instead, they will bake and spoil.

Now for the pastry cases. Preheat the oven to 200°C/400°F/Gas Mark 6. Roll out the pastry 4–5 mm thick and cut it into 4 x 7.5–10 cm rectangles. Sit them on a greaseproof-papered baking tray and chill for 15–20 minutes. Now score them 1 cm in from the edge to create the vol-au-vent. For exact straight rising of the pastry, balance a second baking tray on tartlet tins or small darioles 2 cm above the pastries. Bake for 25–30 minutes. For a shiny finish, take one egg yolk mixed with a drop of milk and brush on top. Place the pastries back in the oven for 2–3 minutes to glaze.

To cook the rhubarb, heat the oven to 160°C/325°F/Gas Mark 3. Peel the rhubarb, if stringy, and cut it into 1 cm chunks. Place it in a roasting tray and sprinkle it with the caster sugar (75 g only may be needed, but if it is sour once cooked, add the rest). Cover with tin foil and cook in the oven for 10 minutes. Once tender, take it out and drain off any juices. (Keep it for the syrup.)

Now make the fool. Purée the 250 g of cooked rhubarb chunks. Once cool, stir into the pastry cream. Lightly whip the double cream and fold it

into the rhubarb mix. Chill: the fool should stay thick and creamy.

Reduce the rhubarb juices by half until you have a thick, sweet syrup.

To assemble the dish, cut away the lid, 1 cm in from the edge, of the vol-au-vent, then remove the pastry from the inside, leaving a crispy pastry case. Spoon the rhubarb compôte into the base, and some fool over it. Lay the dried rhubarb slices carefully over, overlapping them, 6–8 per portion. Drizzle the reduced syrup over and around each tart.

Note: Tinned rhubarb can be used for the compôte and the fool, with the syrup from the tin for drizzling. Tinned custard can replace the Pastry Cream.

Lemon Meringue Pie

Four textures from the three flavours of meringue, lemon curd and the pastry base. All of these flavours hold their own texture, and the meringue is lucky enough to carry two!

   A good meringue has a crispy, firm crust with light, pillowy marshmallow inside. The sweetness of the meringue balances with the acidity of the lemon centre and both are set off by the crisp pastry base. As an alternative, use the Lemon Tart on page 49 as your base. It has a softer, creamier flavour in contrast to the sharp bite of this one. Both work beautifully, especially once finished with a good 'spiky' topping!

Make the filling: bring the water, lemon juice and zest to the boil, then add the butter. Stir into the mix as it melts. Cream together the egg yolks, sugar and cornflour. Then pour the boiled lemon mix on to the egg yolk mix and strain through a sieve. Return to a pan and cook on a low heat until thickened. Spoon it into the cooked pastry case and allow it to cool and set.

Now for the meringue. This recipe is for an Italian meringue, which means that it is made with boiled sugar poured and whisked into whipped egg whites until it is cool, thick and creamy. It has a denser texture than if you whisk together sugar and egg whites in the usual way. You can, however, make a basic meringue for this recipe, using 225 g of caster sugar to 4 egg whites.

Preheat the oven to 220–230°C/425–450°F/Gas Mark 7–8.

Boil the water and sugar together to 129°C. While still whisking, pour on the sugar and continue to whisk until the meringue is thick, creamy and at room temperature. Now spoon, pipe or 'spike' it on top of the lemon filling. Bake for 10–15 minutes or until the spikes are golden.

Note: The meringue can be cooked on 175°C/350°F/Gas Mark 4 for 25–30 minutes for a drier finish, for this alternative the pie will need the curd filling. If you use 7 cm rings, this recipe will make 6–8 individual lemon meringue pies, as featured on the front cover.

The meringue spikes can also be coloured until burnt, which gives a slightly bitter flavour to go with the sweetness of the dish.

Serves 6–8

1 x 20 cm Sweet Pastry case (see page 180), blind-baked or 1 x cooked Lemon Tart (not glazed) (see page 49)

For the filling
175 ml water
140 g caster sugar
35 g cornflour
35 g butter
2 lemons, finely grated and juiced
3 egg yolks

For the meringue
350 g caster sugar
180 ml water
4 large egg whites

Steamed Sponge Puddings

Steamed lemon sponge was the first pudding I made, aged fourteen. It took me all morning, but it was worth every minute: the light lemon-coloured and flavoured sponge with the lemon sauce brought a smile to everyone's face. The real satisfaction, though, was in seeing how much bigger the smiles became when everybody tucked in!

With this recipe I've given a basic ingredients list and several variations so hopefully you'll find one that suits you.

The quantities here will fill a 750 ml pudding basin or 5–6 x 150 ml individual moulds. Plastic moulds are best: you can turn out the puddings easily with a squeeze!

1 x 750 ml pudding basin *or* 5–6 x 150 ml individual moulds, buttered and floured

For the basic sponge
100 g unsalted butter
150 g caster sugar
2 eggs
1 egg yolk
200 g self-raising flour
1–2 tablespoons milk, if needed

Beat the butter and sugar together until almost white and the sugar has dissolved – easily achieved in an electric mixer. Then add an egg and beat until it is completely mixed in and fluffy. Repeat with the other egg and then continue with the egg yolk. An easier way to achieve this is to beat or fork the two eggs lightly with the egg yolk and pour slowly onto the butter mix while it is turning in the mixer. Now fold in the sifted flour until it is completely incorporated, adding the milk if necessary. Spoon into the mould(s) to three-quarters full. Cover with greaseproof paper or tin foil, with a fold in the centre to create space for the rising pudding. Steam over boiling water. Individual puddings take 40 minutes and a large one $1\frac{1}{4}$–$1\frac{1}{2}$ hours. Top up the water as necessary during cooking.

Variations

Steamed Treacle Sponge
Add a generous tablespoon of Lyle's golden syrup to the mix along with a spoonful or two in the base of the moulds. To serve trickle more over the top. This eats best with custard or pouring cream.

Steamed Lemon Sponge
Add the zest and juice of 1 lemon to the pudding mix in place of the milk. For extra lemon flavour, when you have half-filled the moulds, spoon in 1–2 teaspoons of lemon curd and cover it with the rest of the mix. This goes very well with the Lemon Custard (see page 191) and/or Lemon Curd Ice-cream (see page 86).

Steamed Orange Sponge with Hot Orange Sauce

Boil the juice of 3 oranges with the finely grated zest of 1 orange until reduced by two-thirds and cool. Add in place of the milk in the basic recipe. Marmalade Ice-cream (see page 85) goes well with it.

For the hot orange sauce
600 ml orange juice
25–50 g caster sugar
1 teaspoon arrowroot *or* cornflour
1 tablespoon cold water

For the hot orange sauce bring the juice to the boil and reduce it by half. Add the sugar to taste (start with a tablespoon). Mix the arrowroot or cornflour with the cold water and add a few drops to the juice until you have a good coating consistency. Simmer for 2–3 minutes before serving.

Steamed Chocolate Sponge

Replace 50 g of the flour in the basic mix with 50 g cocoa powder. Once the batter is made, grate 50–100 g chocolate into it, then steam as for the basic recipe. To serve, scatter with chocolate shavings (see page 198).

Other ideas

Try a teaspoon of cinnamon in the pudding mix. Then lay some cooked apple pieces (flavoured with cider or Calvados) in the base of the mould before topping with the sponge mix. Cooked rhubarb at the base of a lemon sponge is delicious.

You could mix fresh raspberries with the lemon sponge batter and put more in the base of the mould, then serve it with Raspberry Coulis (see page 190), or spoon some homemade Strawberry or Raspberry Jam (see page 193) into the base of the moulds for a Sticky Lemon and Raspberry Pudding. Other fruits to try: plums, pineapple (with coconut), damsons, apricots, peaches, blackberries, summer fruits, cherries – and more!

Microwave 'Steamed' Treacle Pudding

Quick to make, quick to cook and it works with any of the variations on pages 69–70.

Put the flour, butter, sugar and eggs into a mixer or food-processor, with one tablespoon of the syrup. Blitz until smooth, adding one or two drops of milk, if necessary to give a soft consistency. Pour the remaining syrup into the pudding basin and spoon the mix on top. Cover with cling-film and pierce with a knife.

For a 500-watt microwave, cook on high for 4½–5 minutes (yes, as quick as that!) or until a skewer pushed into the centre of the sponge comes out clean. For every 100 watts above this, reduce the cooking time by 15 seconds. Now all you have to do is turn it out and enjoy it! To serve, spoon a little more syrup on top and eat a steamed sponge that hasn't even been steamed – which must be clever!

Serves 4–6

1 x 750 ml pudding basin, lightly buttered and floured

100 g self-raising flour
100 g butter, softened
100 g caster sugar
2 eggs
2–3 tablespoons Lyle's Golden Syrup

Steamed Bakewell Pudding

The opposite experience to Bakewell Tart Ice-cream on page 102! This is hot and springy – just the thing for Sunday lunch on a chilly day.

Mix together all of the dry ingredients. Then add the egg along with the raspberry jam and the milk to make a loose dough consistency. Spoon the mixture into the pudding basin and cover it lightly with buttered, pleated tin foil. Steam for 1½–2 hours until just firm to touch, checking the hot-water level from time to time. Once cooked, turn out the pudding. If you like, spoon over some warmed jam – the homemade jams on pages 194–6 are particularly good because they are not too firmly set – and sprinkle it with toasted almonds and icing sugar, if using.

Note: The pudding can be made in individual 150 ml moulds, and steamed for 45 minutes to 1 hour. Any other jam, or marmalade, can replace the raspberry.

Serves 4–6

1 x 900 ml–1.2 l pudding basin, buttered and floured
100 g self-raising flour
75 g ground almonds
50 g dried suet
50 g white breadcrumbs
50 g caster sugar
pinch of salt
1 egg
100 g raspberry jam
milk to loosen the mix
flaked almonds (optional)
extra jam for sauce (optional)
icing sugar (optional)

Spotted Dick

I've never been quite sure about the name, but always very sure about the taste. Spotted Dick was a school-dinner pudding I looked forward to. Shame about the lumpy custard! Traditionally, it is a basic suet dough recipe, helped along with currants and sugar. I'm taking it just a short step further with lemon zest for zing!

You can add endless combinations to vary Spotted Dick: orange zest, chocolate, chopped nuts ... Try substituting 50 g of cocoa for 50 g of flour and add some chocolate chips and orange zest along with the currants. Or replace the sugar and half of the milk with 5–6 tablespoons of golden syrup.

Serves 6–8

300 g plain flour
10 g baking powder
150 g shredded suet
75 g caster sugar
100 g currants
finely grated zest of 1–2 lemons
185–200 ml milk

Mix together all the dry ingredients with the currants and lemon zest. Pour in 185 ml of the milk and stir together, adding more milk if necessary to give a binding/dropping consistency. The wetter the mix the moister the sponge. Roll the mix into a 15–20 cm x 5 cm diameter cylinder, wrap it in buttered greaseproof paper, with a fold to allow space for the sponge to rise, and tie the paper at both ends. Put it in a hot steamer and cook for about 1 hour. Remove the paper and slice the pudding into portions. I find it's best to cut the slices approximately 2.5 cm thick for a good texture. Spotted Dick goes very well with Sauce Anglaise (see page 191), perhaps a little trickle of honey or golden syrup too!

Fried Spotted Dick Slice

A great way to use up any Spotted Dick. In fact, it's so good you might find yourself making Spotted Dick just to try this recipe too. I made it originally with brioche, which was brilliant to eat.

4 eggs
4 tablespoons caster sugar
4 tablespoons double cream
6–8 slices Spotted Dick
50 g butter

Whisk together the eggs, sugar and cream, then soak the Spotted Dick slices in it for approximately 5 minutes on each side. Melt the butter in a warm frying pan and fry the slices on a medium heat for 4–5 minutes on each side until they are golden. They eat well with thick cream and, perhaps, a good spoonful of homemade jam.

Steamed Apricot and Orange Nutty Pudding

This was cooked for me at a friend's dinner party – I just had to have the recipe! It was served with Chantilly Cream (see page 185) mixed with a little sour cream – a great combination.

Chop the dried apricots into small dice. Cream together the sugar and butter. Add the egg, followed by the flour and the bicarbonate of soda. Then fold in the nuts, the chopped apricots and the marmalade, and stir in the milk. Spoon the mixture into the pudding basin. Cover it with greaseproof paper, with a fold to allow space for rising, and steam for 1½–2 hours. Serve with the Orange Custard on page 191, or with the Hot Orange Sauce on page 70, flavoured with Grand Marnier or Cointreau.

Note: Lemon or lime marmalade can be used in place of orange.

Serves 4–6

1 x 900 ml–1.2 l pudding basin, greased and floured

150 g ready-to-eat dried apricots
125 g light soft brown sugar
125 g butter
1 egg, beaten
150 g plain flour, sifted
1 teaspoon bicarbonate of soda
50 g nibbed almonds (mixed chopped hazelnuts *or* walnuts can also be used)
150 g orange marmalade
175 ml milk

Sticky Toffee Pudding

Serves 6–8

1 x 22.5 cm square baking tin
   (28 cm x 20 cm will also work),
   buttered and/or lined with
   greaseproof paper

175 g dates, stoned and chopped
300 ml water
1 teaspoon bicarbonate of soda
50 g unsalted butter
175 g caster sugar
2 eggs, beaten
175 g self-raising flour
1 teaspoon vanilla essence

For the sauce
300 ml double cream
50 g Demerara sugar
2 teaspoons black treacle

One of Britain's richest desserts. It holds everything its title declares. It's very sticky with an amazing toffee flavour, and as for the toffee sauce, it just dribbles over the black treacle, working beautifully with the cream and Demerara sugar. A pudding we just have to treat ourselves to – an eating experience!

Preheat the oven to 180°C/350°F/Gas Mark 4.

Boil the dates in the water for about 5 minutes until soft. Add the bicarbonate of soda, and keep the dates in the water. Cream together the butter and sugar until light and fluffy, then add the eggs and beat well. Mix in the dates (with the water), the flour and the vanilla essence, then pour into the baking tin. Bake for 35–40 minutes until just firm to the touch.

To make the sauce, place all of the ingredients in a saucepan over a low heat and stir together until blended, then bring to the boil. Cut the pudding into portions and ladle over the sauce.

Note: I use medjool dates in this recipe. They come from India and, without doubt, are the best to eat. They have a natural fudge-toffee flavour that is perfect for this dish, but other varieties can also be used. You will find a recipe for Sticky Toffee Pudding Ice-cream on page 101. The idea for the ice-cream came from this recipe, so if you're a real Sticky Toffee Pudding freak then why not serve the ice-cream with this too? That'll put you in a really sticky situation!

Sussex Pond Pudding

This pudding can only be described as a total experience. It's a steamed suet pudding filled with a pierced whole lemon, butter and sugar. As the pudding cooks, the lemon juices are released into the butter and sugar, making a caramelised lemon sauce that floods out when the pudding is cut – which is where the pond comes in.

Sift the flour with the salt and mix in the suet. Add the milk and water to form a soft dough. Wrap it in clingfilm and leave it to rest in the refrigerator for 30 minutes. Then roll three-quarters of the dough – the rest of it is for the lid – to about 5 mm thickness.

Serves 4–6

1 x 1.2–1.5 l pudding basin, buttered

225 g self-raising flour
100 g dried suet
pinch of salt
120–150 ml milk and water, mixed
100 g unsalted butter
100 g light soft brown sugar
1 whole lemon

Line the pudding basin with the dough, pushing out any creases. Cut the butter into dice and place half, along with half of the sugar, in the bowl. Pierce the lemon with a small sharp knife or skewer and sit it on top of the other ingredients. Scatter the remaining butter and sugar over the lemon. Now roll out the remaining dough into the lid. Put it on top, and pinch all around to seal in the flavours. Cover with buttered and pleated tin foil to allow for rising during cooking.

Steam for 4 hours, checking the hot-water level from time to time. Once cooked, allow the pudding to rest in the basin for 6–8 minutes before turning it out into a large serving bowl. When you cut it, your home will be filled with the fragrance of lemon! Sussex Pond Pudding lives on!

Christmas Pudding

Do we ever finish it? What normally happens is that we all tuck into a rich starter, and follow it with roast turkey or pork, stuffing, bacon, chipolatas, roast potatoes, three or four veg and something more. It's true, isn't it? I'm not exaggerating! When the Christmas pudding arrives (usually on fire!) everyone says, 'Just a small piece – no, half of that!' Yes?

So why am I including this recipe? Well, it's just too good to miss!

I like to make my Christmas Pudding well ahead of time, usually around August: this gives it time to mature. I keep the raw mixture refrigerated for at least a week before cooking, which gives the flavours time to blend together. Happy Christmas Pud!

Sift the flour with the baking powder. Add the breadcrumbs, suet, ground almonds, soft dark brown sugar and spices. Mince the prunes and carrots together through a medium blade and add to the mix with the dried fruit, mixed peel, apples, lemon and orange zest. Beat the eggs and stir into the pudding mix with the lemon and orange juice, rum, treacle, golden syrup and stout. You should now have pudding mixture of approximately 3 kg in total weight. It will have a reasonably moist and loose texture but if it appears dry add some more stout and rum. Leave for a minimum of 24 hours, but preferably for a week. Then taste it to check for full flavour and richness. If it's bland, add some more spices to liven it up.

To cook the puddings, butter and lightly flour 3 x 900 g pudding basins. Fill each three-quarters full with the mix, top with a circle of greaseproof paper then cover with parchment paper, muslin or tin foil and tie it on firmly, leaving a fold to give the pudding room to rise. Steam over boiling water for 4–6 hours (6 hours will make the puddings even richer). Don't forget to top up the water from time to time.

Leave the puddings to cool before refrigerating or storing them in a cold dark place.

To serve the puddings on the Big Day, they will need a minimum of 1 hour (preferably 1½–2, which will make them richer) to return them to a tender pudding texture. I like to serve rum- or brandy-flavoured Sauce Anglaise (see page 191) with Christmas Pudding, along with lots of pouring cream – well, it is Christmas!

Makes 3 x 900 g puddings

225 g plain flour
1 teaspoon baking powder
225 g fresh white breadcrumbs
225 g shredded suet
100 g ground almonds
500 g soft dark brown sugar
1 teaspoon mixed spice
½ teaspoon grated nutmeg
½ teaspoon cinnamon
175 g stoned prunes
175 g carrots, peeled
750 g mixed currants, sultanas, raisins
50 g chopped mixed peel
2 apples, peeled, cored and roughly chopped
juice and grated zest of 1 orange
juice and grated zest of 1 lemon
5 eggs
100–150 ml rum
4 tablespoons black treacle
4 tablespoons golden syrup
300 ml stout

Griddled Lemon Scones

Makes around 20 scones. Just not enough!

450 g self-raising flour, plus extra for dusting

100 g butter, plus extra for frying

175 g currants and sultanas mixed

grated zest of 1 lemon

100 g caster sugar

2 eggs

2–4 tablespoons milk

Here are some scones with a difference. They are griddled in a frying pan rather than being baked, which gives them quite a different texture. The lemon zest provides a soft, acidic, perfumed flavour. These scones are delicious with strawberry or raspberry jam, page 193. Both fruits have a close relationship with lemon -- they always get on and will never fall out! Try the scones as a pudding, with clotted cream and fresh strawberries.

Sift the flour, then rub in the butter. Fold in the currants and sultanas with the lemon zest and sugar. Make a well in the centre, add the eggs, 2 tablespoons of the milk and mix to a soft dough. If it feels too dry, add the remaining 2 tablespoons of milk.

Roll out the dough 1 cm thick on a flour-dusted surface and cut out the scones into 6 cm rounds.

Warm a frying pan to a medium heat and cook the scones in a little butter for 4–5 minutes on each side until golden brown. They are best served warm but can also be eaten cold.

Note: For a richer lemon flavour, use the zest of two lemons. For 'St Clements' scones add the grated zest of half a large or 1 small orange to the zest of 1 lemon. Or omit the lemon zest and add a teaspoon of cinnamon or mixed spice instead.

Lemon Posset

This pudding has to be one of the easiest of all time to prepare and cook! Looking at the ingredients it's quite hard to believe that the recipe will work – how will it set? The three simple ingredients are cooked together, the sugar and acidity of the lemon juice react with the cream so that once it has cooled and been refrigerated it sets just like a mousse. Here's the 'difficult' recipe!

Serves 6

6 wine glasses

900 ml double cream
225–250 g caster sugar
juice of 3 lemons

Bring the cream and sugar to the boil and simmer for 2–3 minutes. Add the lemon juice and mix in well. Remove from the heat and leave to cool slightly before pouring it into the glasses, leaving a 1 cm space at the top of each glass. These can now be refrigerated and allowed to set which will take between 2–3 hours.

I like to pour some liquid cream on top of each Posset – it helps to balance the rich acidic lemon flavour.

Ice-creams

I could write a whole book on ice-creams! The variations and combinations are endless! The basic Vanilla Ice-cream (page 84) can be used as a base for many more flavours, or use a bought one. I recommend using an ice-cream machine for the best results: as it churns, the mixture becomes lighter and the texture even smoother. Fill the machine half to two-thirds full, to give room for the mixture to increase in volume. If you don't have a machine you can still make the ices: freeze the mix and whisk it every 20–30 minutes until it is set. It will still taste good. All of the ice-cream recipes can be made with whipping cream in place of double cream, and tinned custard instead of fresh. Fruit-based ice-creams are best made from a fruit coulis (see page 190), mixed with crème fraîche and yoghurt (as for the Lemon Curd recipe, page 196). Then all you have to do is churn it! It's a good idea to make all ice-cream 24 hours in advance of when you plan to eat them so that they have plenty of time to set.

Look out for my new version of 'The Classics', on pages 93–107. I've taken traditional British puddings and turned them into ice-creams. Paradise. They keep their original flavours, but at a very different temperature! Sweet dreams are made of this!

Vanilla Ice-cream

Makes 750–900 ml

300 ml double cream
300 ml milk
1 vanilla pod *or* a few drops
   strong vanilla essence
6 egg yolks
175 g caster sugar

Do use fresh vanilla pods for the ultimate vanilla flavour – once split and infused with the cream, you are left with the most amazing aroma of the spice – or keep some in a jar of caster sugar and use it in this recipe. If you can't get the pods, use a few drops of strong vanilla essence.

Mix together the cream and milk in a saucepan. Split the vanilla pod and scrape the 'seeds' into the cream (or add the essence). Put in the pan and bring to the boil. While the cream mix is heating, whisk the egg yolks and sugar until they form thick ribbons – you can do this in a food-processor. Pour on the cream and stir until well blended. Cook in the bowl over a pan of simmering water, stirring, until the custard coats the back of a spoon. (Do not let it boil – or the eggs will scramble.) Strain through a sieve; discard the vanilla pod. Leave to cool, stirring from time to time to prevent a skin forming. You will need to churn the ice-cream in two batches. Pour in the first half and churn for 20 minutes until it has thickened and increased in volume. Repeat with the second batch. It's important not to churn it until it is completely frozen or it will take on a curdled, slightly grainy texture. Pour the ice-cream into a container and put it in the freezer, to finish setting. This will guarantee a lovely silky-smooth consistency.

Note: Lots of other flavours can be added to this base or to the Quick Vanilla Ice-cream, such as: marmalade; golden syrup; honey; chocolate; liqueurs; mashed banana to name but a few.

Quick Vanilla Ice-cream

a dash or two of vanilla essence
1 x 425 g carton *or* can ready-
   made custard
150 ml double cream

The speed is in the making, rather than the freezing!

Mix the vanilla essence with the ready-made custard. Lightly whip the cream to soft peaks, and then fold it gently into the custard. Taste for sweetness. If it is a little dull, stir in icing sugar to taste. Put it in an airtight container and freeze, stirring from time to time for a lighter finish.

Variations

Banana Ice-cream

Mix the lemon juice with the chopped bananas to help them keep their colour. Add the bananas and liqueur to the vanilla base and liquidise. Push through a sieve and churn as for Vanilla Ice-cream. Pour into an airtight container and freeze.

1 quantity vanilla base (see page 84)
225 g bananas, peeled and chopped
few drops lemon juice
2 tablespoons banana liqueur

Chocolate Ice-cream

Add the chocolate to the vanilla base and stir until melted. Churn and finish as Vanilla Ice-cream.

1 quantity vanilla base (see page 84), made with 100 g of caster sugar and omitting the vanilla pod
175–225 g good quality plain chocolate, grated

Marmalade Ice-cream

Follow the vanilla base recipe. Stir the boiled cream and milk into the egg yolks and sugar, then add the marmalade and continue as the method for Vanilla Ice-cream.

1 quantity vanilla base (see page 84), made with 100 g caster sugar and omitting the vanilla pod
1 x 350 g jar fine or coarse marmalade

Brown Sugar Ice-cream

Follow the basic vanilla recipe but substitute light or dark soft brown sugar for the caster. Delicious with pouring cream on its own, or as an accompaniment to steamed sponges, barbecued bananas, baked apples and more.

Fresh Mint Ice-cream

Makes 650–800 ml

250 ml whipping cream
250 ml milk
4 full stems fresh mint
6 egg yolks
200 g caster sugar
5 tablespoons crème de menthe

This ice-cream is a great accompaniment for the mint syrup Babas, on page 140–1. You could add some chocolate chips towards the end of churning, and hot Bitter Chocolate Sauce (see page 192) is delicious with it.

Bring the cream, milk and mint to the boil. Remove from the heat and leave to infuse for 20 minutes. Whisk the egg yolks and sugar together until pale, light and creamy. Re-heat and strain the minted cream on to the egg mix, whisking continuously. Now cook it on a low heat, or in a bowl over simmering water, until it coats the back of a spoon. Remove from the heat, add the crème de menthe and leave to cool. Churn it in an ice-cream machine for 20–25 minutes, until thick and creamy. Pour it into a suitable container and freeze to finish setting.

Lemon Curd and Soft Fruit Purée Flavour Ice-creams

Makes 400–500 ml

½ quantity lemon curd (see page 196) *or* 1 x 350 g jar lemon curd (use the same quantity of fruit purée)
2 large tablespoons crème fraîche
1 large tablespoon natural yoghurt

The easiest of all to make! Buy a jar of lemon curd, if you don't want to make it. Blitz tinned fruits in the food-processor to a purée unless you want to cook fresh. However you do it, it's simple and tasty!

Mix the lemon curd or fruit purée with the crème fraîche and yoghurt, and churn into a smooth ice-cream. That's it!

Note: The recipe works equally well with Orange Curd (see Note, page 196).

Quick Cheesecake Ice-cream

This ice-cream doesn't need a machine and, once in the freezer, no whisking either. Present it either on a digestive biscuit base or with the biscuit mix crumbled on top. It's quick, easy and so good!

Beat the cream cheese until soft. Stir in the custard. In a saucepan, boil the water and sugar to 129°C. Whisk the egg whites to soft peaks and slowly pour the hot syrup on to them, whisking vigorously – this is best achieved in a food-processor or mixer. Continue to whisk on a medium speed until the meringue is at room temperature. Now fold it into the cream cheese mix.

Mix the melted butter with the crumbled biscuits, and if you are making the full cheesecake, press them down firmly on the base of the tin. If the crumbs are for sprinkling, chill them to set the butter. Top the base with the cheesecake mix and freeze for several hours, or pour it into a suitable container, and freeze.

When ready to serve, remove the cheesecake ice-cream from the tin and decorate it with the topping of your choice.

Note: I like to serve this with homemade jams (see page 193). Put a spoonful or two of the jam on a plate or in a bowl. Scroll a portion of the ice-cream on top and sprinkle over the coarse crumbled biscuit.

   The juice of a lemon can be added to the cheesecake mix – particularly good if you are serving it with raspberries or strawberries.

Serves 4–6

1 x 15 cm loose-bottomed cake
   tin *or* open ring deep flan tin,
   lined with greaseproof paper

400 g cream cheese
300 ml tin *or* carton custard
175 g caster sugar
85 ml water
2 egg whites

For the biscuit base/topping
180–200 g digestive biscuits,
   crumbled
25–30 g melted butter
(You will need the greater
   quantities for a base, less for
   sprinkling.)

For the topping/accompaniment
raspberries; strawberries;
   passionfruit; *or* tinned
   blackcurrant pie filling

Exotic Fruit Sorbet

The flavour of the sorbet is as exciting as the fruits themselves. They are being helped along with a drop of Malibu – it's not essential, but does help. There's no syrup being used as a base here; the fruits with the sugar create their own. This is a great dessert for summer – or any other time of the year! It's also good as a pre-pudding course to cleanse and liven up your palate for whatever comes next.

Quarter the pineapple, cut away the core, and chop it into small rough dice. Place the pieces in a saucepan with 1 tablespoon of the sugar. Cook on a medium heat for 5–6 minutes until tender. Leave to cool. While the pineapple is cooking, remove the stone and seeds from the mango and melons, and chop them into rough dice. Halve the passionfruits and scoop out the flesh. Put all the fruit into the food-processor, including the pineapple, with the Malibu (if using) and 150 g of the sugar. Blitz to a purée. This will also dissolve the sugar. Taste for sweetness and, if necessary, add the remaining sugar and blitz again. Strain the purée through a sieve, then churn the sorbet mix until it has thickened and is almost creamy. Pour it into a suitable container and freeze to finish setting.

This sorbet can be served as it is, or in a tuile basket (see page 178) surrounded by a glorious selection of exotic fruits.

Note: A rich exotic fruit coulis complements this sorbet perfectly.

Makes approximately 1 litre

1 mango, skinned
2 small melons, preferably Cantaloupe, skinned
1 small pineapple, skinned
10 passionfruit
150–200 g caster sugar
25 ml Malibu (optional)

Melon Soup Sorbet

Serves 6–8

3 medium-sized ripe melons,
   Charentais, Cantaloupe, Ogen
   or Honeydew will all work
150 g caster sugar

This dish makes either a fabulous starter or a dessert. I like to use a mixture of three different melons: their colours look pretty together and the flavours contrast too. The orange-coloured Charentais melon, Cantaloupe and Ogen, tend to give the best flavours.

Halve and seed all the melons. Use a melon baller to scoop out the flesh of one melon, or if you are using 3 different ones, scoop some balls from half of each. Cut each half melon into quarters, then cut away all the flesh, including the trimmings from the balled melon. Place all of the flesh with the sugar into a food-processor or liquidizer and blitz to a purée. This quantity of sugar should be plenty to sweeten and to make the sorbet smooth, but taste and add more, if necessary, then blitz again.

Pour the mix into the ice-cream machine and churn to a thick 'slush' consistency, 10–15 minutes: the sorbet soup should be thick, but by no means set. Garnish with the melon balls, and maybe a few fine strands of mint.

Note: If you wish to make the soup in advance, churn it until it has thickened, then freeze. When you need it, remove it from the freezer 10–15 minutes before serving. Once it has softened lightly, blitz it in a food-processor to return it to a smooth thick consistency. If you do not have an ice-cream machine, just make up the mix and freeze it. When it is needed, blitz it in a food-processor. Or, simply chill the melon mix to serve as a cool melon soup rather than a frozen one. The melons can be halved and scooped/ spooned out; then use the shells to serve the soup in. The soup can be made into a firm sorbet by continuing to churn until it is almost set.

Damson Sorbet

As a child I often went damson picking (I never ate them while I picked – they're far too sour – I saved that for strawberries) and brought them home to my mother. Inspired by her wonderful crumbles, pies and jams, I turned them into this sorbet, which is packed with autumn flavour.

Wash the fresh damsons and remove the stones. Place the fruit in a saucepan and cover with the stock syrup. Bring to a simmer and cook for 5 minutes until the fruit is tender. Remove from the heat and blitz it to a purée. Stir in the lemon juice and strain through a sieve. Allow the sorbet mix to cool, then churn in an ice-cream machine for 20–25 minutes until thickened. Pour it into a suitable container and leave it to finish setting in the freezer.

Note: If you don't have an ice-cream maker, freeze the sorbet and whisk it occasionally until it is set. Then remove it from the freezer and blitz it to a thick purée before refreezing it.

Makes approximately 600-800 ml

675 g fresh *or* frozen damsons (500 g if already stoned)
250 ml stock syrup (see page 188)
2 teaspoons lemon juice

Port and Lemon Sorbet

This sorbet is the perfect partner for Upside Down Fig Pudding on page 44 or for grilled sweet figs: halve the figs, sprinkle them with a little soft brown sugar, and caramelise under the grill until bubbling and golden. Serve with the sorbet just melting over the top.

Using a potato peeler, remove the zest from 2 of the lemons, making sure there is no white pith left on it as this will make the sorbet bitter. Add the zest to the syrup and bring it to the boil. Remove it from the heat and add the juice from all 3 lemons. Leave to cool. Add the port and continue to infuse for 1–2 hours. Then strain the mixture and churn it in an ice-cream maker for 20–25 minutes. Five minutes before the end of the churning, lightly whisk to break up the egg white, add it to the sorbet and continue to churn. Pour the sorbet into a suitable container and put it in the freezer to finish setting.

Makes approximately 600 ml

zest and juice of 3 lemons
250 ml stock syrup (see page 188)
100 ml port
1 egg white

Gooseberry Sherbet

Serves 4–6

450 g fresh *or* frozen
  gooseberries
250 ml stock syrup (see page
  188)
250 ml milk
1 teaspoon lemon juice
1 egg white

Sherbets are not the same as sorbets. A sorbet is made from fruit purée mixed with sweet stock syrup and that's basically it, while a sherbet uses those ingredients plus milk and egg white, which give it a fizzy finish. Almost any other fruit, fresh or frozen, can replace the gooseberries.

Wash the fresh gooseberries, put them in a saucepan with the stock syrup and bring to a simmer. Cover and cook gently for 3–4 minutes or until the fruit is tender. Remove from the heat and leave to cool. Now purée the gooseberries in the syrup and strain them through a sieve. Stir in the milk and lemon juice, then pour the mixture into an ice-cream machine and begin to churn. It will take between 20–25 minutes to reach a thick almost setting stage. When ready, whisk the egg white to soft peaks and add it to the mix. Store the sherbet in the freezer until you need it – or eat it straight away.

Note: If you do not have an ice-cream maker, freeze the sherbet before adding the egg white, whisking every so often to break the ice crystals. Once it has frozen, put it into a food-processor and blitz it to a purée. Then fold in the beaten egg white and refreeze.

The Classics

Here are the classics, exciting to make, serve and eat! Tell your friends that dessert is going to be a Bakewell Tart, then place Bakewell Tart Ice-cream in front of them that looks so stunning, I'm pretty sure they'll be after a second slice! As for the Apple Pie – cut into a crispy pastry that looks like nothing but a hot pie from the oven yet is filled with warm cooked apples and a rich ice-cream – a whole new experience! Here, Steamed Treacle or Golden Syrup Pudding has become an ice-cream, dribbling with extra syrup and thick cream. There's Peach Melba – a large peach-shaped ball of peach ice-cream, sitting on fresh raspberries (pictured below). Or the Iced Black Forest Snowballs – cherry and kirsch ice-cream rolled and passed through rich chocolate!

I think I've said enough – here are the recipes for these and more too.

A melting experience ...

Iced Black Forest Snowballs

The Black Forest connection here is the marriage of Griottine cherries (tinned can be used) and kirsch to flavour the vanilla ice-cream. Then the snowballs are rolled in melted, rich, strong chocolate ... This dish can be lifted even higher with the cherries in syrup from the Warm Black Forest Gâteau recipe on page 150–1, served just warm.

Serves 4–6

250 ml milk
250 ml double cream
1 vanilla pod, split
100 g caster sugar
6 egg yolks
100 g Griottine cherries (see page 10)
300–500 g plain chocolate, grated
50 ml kirsch
cocoa and icing sugar (optional)

Bring the milk and cream to the boil with the vanilla pod. While it is heating whisk the egg yolks and sugar until they form ribbons. Pour the boiled milk on to the eggs, whisking vigorously, and cook on a gentle heat or in a bowl over a pan of simmering water, stirring, until the custard coats the back of the spoon. Don't let it boil. Remove from the heat and leave to cool, then churn the custard for 20–25 minutes until it has increased in volume and thickness. Add the whole Griottines for the last few turns to spread them into the mix. Pour the ice-cream into a suitable container and leave it in the freezer until well firmed. (You may have to churn the ice-cream in two loads, if the machine isn't big enough to accommodate the whole lot at once.)

Once set, make the snowballs: scoop balls of ice-cream from the mix, sit them on a clingfilmed tray or plate and refreeze. Meanwhile, melt the chocolate in a bowl over warm water: 300 g is enough for one coating, 500 g for a double thick coat. Stick a fork into each ball and dip in the chocolate. Allow any excess to roll off and quickly place the ball on a clean tray, then remove the fork. The chocolate will set over the fork holes. You could also use tongs, or even dip by hand. Now refreeze, and repeat, if you'd prefer a thicker coating.

Dust each plate lightly with cocoa and icing sugar, sit the snowballs on top and dust them too. Decorate with fresh cherries, if available (if they have stalks, you could dip them in caramel and sit a pair at the top of each plate), or with the cherries from the Warm Black Forest Gâteau, and some cream – pouring, thick, clotted or Chantilly – it's up to you!

Apple Pie and Apple Crumble Ice-creams

Here are two ideas from the same concept. They can both be as easy to prepare as you please. The apple purée and chunky cooked apple can both be bought in jars, which cuts out a lot of preparation. Although making anything fresh brings extra flavour and more personal satisfaction, I have used the jarred products myself and they give very good results. The puréed and chunky apple are the same recipe. The purée simply means that you've blitzed the chunky!

Both dishes are best served with a warm Sauce Anglaise (see page 191) or pouring cream. The warm custard just helps melt the whole experience. For the apple pie, the apple wedges are totally optional, but they give a lovely bitter-sweet warm flavour to add to the dish.

Apple Pie Ice-cream

A large apple pie sitting on the table looks quite stunning – and when you cut into it and ice-cream starts to trickle out ... delicious. Sauce Anglaise, served warm, provides the classic finishing touch. If you don't want to go to the trouble of making the whole dish, the tangy Apple Ice-cream is excellent on its own, or served in tuile baskets (see page 178).

First make the apple purée. Cut the Bramleys into rough 5 mm dice. Melt the butter in a large saucepan and add the apples, sugar and lemon juice. Cook on a medium heat until tender and just starting to break down. Remove from the heat. Spoon away two-thirds – about 700 g – liquidise, then sieve to a smooth purée. Reserve the 300 g of chunky apple. (It is not essential to purée the apple for the ice-cream, you can leave it chunky for added apple texture if your prefer. A little Calvados or reduced sweet cider adds extra flavour.)

Now make the ice-cream. Mix together all the ingredients and churn in an ice-cream machine for 20–25 minutes. For a large pie, freeze it in the slightly smaller cake tin so that it will fit into the pastry case. For individual pies, set the ice-creams in the 4 x 7 cm x 4 cm rings. Fill them, leaving a 5 mm–1 cm gap from the top and freeze. Leftover ice-cream can be frozen in a suitable container and offered separately with the pies.

For the pastry cases, preheat the oven to 200°C/400°F/Gas Mark 6. Roll the pastry to 2–3 mm thick and use it to line the larger metal pastry rings or the large tin. Then line them with greaseproof paper and baking beans. Cut out the lids, using one of the metal rings as a cutter, and make leaves as decorations from the trimmings. Sit the pastry cases on a greased baking tray. Lay the lids over a few baking beans on the baking tray – as they cook they will shape themselves around the beans, which gives the finished pies the traditionally uneven bumpy top! Stick on the leaves, brush the lids with milk and sprinkle with granulated sugar for the classic finish. Bake for 20 minutes until crispy and golden. Remove from the oven, take out the paper and beans from the pastry cases and leave to cool. Allow the lids to cool over the beans.

For the apple wedge garnish, cut the Granny Smith into eighths. Melt the

Serves 4

4 x approximately 8 cm x 4 cm metal rings *or* 1 x approximately 18cm round cake tin for the pastry
4 x approximately 7 cm x 4 cm metal rings *or* 1 x approximately 15 cm round cake tin for the ice-cream

For the apple purée
4 large Bramley apples, peeled and cored
180 g caster sugar
juice of 1 lemon
knob of butter

For the apple ice-cream
700 g apple purée (see above)
4 tablespoons crème fraîche
2 tablespoons natural yoghurt

For the pies
300 g sweet shortcrust pastry (see page 180)
milk for brushing
granulated sugar for sprinkling

For the garnish (optional)
1 large Granny Smith apple

butter in a frying pan and add the apple slices. Fry for 2–3 minutes until the apples are taking on a golden colour. Sprinkle with the caster sugar and allow to caramelise. If the sugar solidifies, add a dessertspoon of water, which will release and dissolve the sugar over the apples.

The pies *must* be assembled at the last minute. Have the cases just warm. Warm the chunky apple, too, and spoon a little into the base of each case. Sit an ice-cream disc on top, finish with more chunky apple, top with a lid, and garnish with apple wedges, if using. Offer cream or Sauce Anglaise (see page 191) separately.

Note: Other flavours can be added: cinnamon and raisins or sultanas can be mixed into the chunky apple for Dutch Apple Tarts, or grated lemon or orange zest for citrus sharpness.

Quick Apple Ice-cream

2 egg whites
100 g caster sugar
250 g jar Bramley apple purée
250 g tinned custard

Ice-cream that doesn't need a machine! Use the recipe with any fruit, keeping to the same proportion given below. The liqueur of your chosen fruit will enhance its flavour. This Apple Ice-cream can be used in the Apple Pie and Apple Crumble recipes on pages 97 and 99. It's also good to eat on its own with tuiles (see page 178), which can be flavoured with a pinch of cinnamon, or try it with Apple Soup on page 142 instead of the sorbet.

Whisk the egg whites with half of the sugar to soft peaks. Add the remaining sugar and continue to whisk until you have a firm meringue. Whisk together the apple purée with the custard. Lightly fold in the meringue and spoon into a suitable container. Freeze until set.

Note: If you are concerned about using the raw meringue in this recipe then follow the recipe for Italian meringue on page 186, which is made with boiled sugar that 'cooks' the egg white.

Apple Crumble
Ice-cream

I prefer to make this in a classic crumble dish, which is presented at the table along with a sauceboat of custard. When you cut into it, the secret is revealed! Happy melting!

Preheat the oven to 200°C/400°F/Gas Mark 6.

Rub the butter into the flour. Once it looks like crumbs add the sugar and almonds. Rub again, until the mix becomes lumpy. This gives you a chunky, coarse crumble. Sprinkle it on to a baking tray and bake for 10–20 minutes, turning occasionally, until crunchy and golden. Remove from the oven and leave to cool.

Spread the ice-cream into a serving dish and smooth the top. Freeze. Remove it from the freezer 10 minutes before serving to thaw a little. Meanwhile warm the chunky apples and the crumble topping. Spoon the chunky apples on top of the ice-cream, then quickly sprinkle over the crumble and serve immediately with pouring cream or custard (or both!).

Note: Any fruit-flavoured ice-cream can be used for this recipe. Blackberries can be warmed with the chunky apples to give you an Apple and Blackberry Crumble Ice-cream.

Serves 4–6

For the crumble mix
75 g butter
100 g plain flour
50 g Demerara sugar
50 g nibbed almonds

1 quantity Apple Ice-cream (see pages 97-8)
1 quantity chunky apple (approximately 300 g), remaining from the Apple Purée (see page 97)

Peach Melba Ice-cream

Serves 4–6

500 g tinned peaches, halves *or* segments
150 g crème fraîche
100 g natural yoghurt
75 ml peach schnapps *or* peach brandy (optional)
grenadine and orange colouring (optional)
175–225 g fresh raspberries
150–175 ml raspberry coulis (see page 190)
Chantilly Cream (see page 185)

Peach Melba is another classic I can't leave alone – it's featured again on page 130 with Roasted Peach Melba. This recipe gives you the opposite of that one! The ice-cream is scooped into a ball, then shaped with a warm knife to look like a fresh peach. With fresh raspberries and a spoonful of Chantilly Cream, Peach Melba is reborn.

Drain the peaches, keeping the syrup to one side. Purée them in a food-processor, then push through a sieve. Now stir in the schnapps with the crème fraîche and yoghurt. For a richer peach colour, add a few drops of grenadine and orange colouring. If grenadine is unavailable, then a dot or two of cochineal (see page 13) will give an orangy-pink finish. Churn the ice-cream mix until thick and increased in volume. Remove from the machine and leave to set in the freezer for a few hours. Then scoop out large balls and lay on a clingfilmed tray. Refreeze. Once firm, smooth with a warm palette knife, making a crease to re-create the natural peach shape. Refreeze until needed.

To serve, take a bowl or a martini-style cocktail glass, stir the raspberries into the coulis and divide between each bowl or glass. Sit an iced peach on top. Spoon a little of the retained peach syrup over each peach for a fresh glossy look. Serve the Chantilly cream separately or spoon some on top.

The ice-cream can be made with 250 g of crème fraîche, omitting the natural yoghurt, or use sour cream instead of crème fraîche. Good-quality raspberry sauces/coulis are available ready-made if you are stuck for time. The Raspberry Jam on page 193 can be used in place of the fresh raspberries and coulis.

Sticky Toffee Pudding Ice-cream

Sticky Toffee Pudding is in the premier dessert division, and this variation on the theme is right up there with the stars! I serve it straight, in a bowl or glass, with a toffee sauce poured over, just like the classic hot pudding.

Boil the cream and milk with the chopped dates. Whisk the egg yolks and sugar until they form ribbons. Pour the boiled cream on to the egg mixture and whisk it in. Cook over a pan of simmering water until it coats the back of a spoon – do not boil! Add the softened toffee, stirring until it is well mixed in. Leave to cool, then pass through a sieve and discard the dates. Now churn the mixture until it has thickened to almost setting point. For the last few turns in the machine, add the dried sugar dates. Pour into an airtight container and put in the freezer to finish setting. It goes beautifully with Caramel Sauce (see page 192), Toffee Cream (see page 187), or melted rich sweet bought toffees. All of the sauces are best served warm.

Note: This ice-cream makes a brilliant accompaniment for crumbles, pies and steamed puddings. Or even serve with the pudding itself (see page 76)! If you can't get the dried sugar dates, which are available in some delicatessens, replace with medjool dates.

Serves 6–8

500 ml double *or* whipping cream
500 ml milk
200 g chopped dates
12 egg yolks
100 g caster sugar
1 x 394 g tin condensed milk toffee (see page 187)
250 g dried sugar dates, chopped

Bakewell Tart Ice-cream

Serves 6

6 x 10 cm diameter x 1–2.5 cm
   deep tartlet cases

For the almond ice-cream
300 ml double cream
300 ml milk
100 g ground almonds
8 egg yolks
120 g caster sugar
50 ml Amaretto (see page 204)
½ quantity sweet shortcrust
   pastry (see page 180)
225 g fresh raspberries
150 ml raspberry coulis (see
   page 190)

For the lemon water icing
finely grated zest and juice ½–1
   lemon
100–150 g icing sugar

Bakewell Tart is a great favourite: the frangipane sponge is so flavoursome and moist from the almond oil. Quite a challenge to simulate that taste in an ice-cream – but it works! All of that flavour is here. Crisp pastry tartlets, raspberries bound in their own coulis, almond ice-cream and just a touch of lemon water icing. The complete Bakewell classic in a completely new form.

Preheat the oven to 200°C/400°F/Gas Mark 6.

First, make the ice-cream. Bring to the boil the cream, milk and almonds. Whisk the egg yolks, sugar and Amaretto until ribbons form. Pour the cream mixture over the eggs and cook in a bowl over simmering water until it coats the back of a spoon. Leave to cool. Then strain through a sieve, and churn in an ice-cream machine for 20–25 minutes. When it has thickened and increased in volume, pour into a container and freeze until set.

While the ice-cream is churning, roll the pastry to 3 mm thick, use it to line the tartlet cases. Then line the cases with greaseproof paper and baking beans and bake for 15–20 minutes, until crispy and golden.

Make the lemon water icing just before you assemble the tarts. Whisk the lemon juice and zest into the icing sugar. Strain out the zest if you prefer a smoother finish.

To build the tart, pipe or drizzle a little lemon icing across the plate, then spoon a little into the base of each pastry case. Sit the cases in the centre of the plates on top of the icing. Stir together the raspberries and the coulis then divide, either warmed or left cold, between the tartlets. Now scroll or scoop the almond ice-cream on top of the raspberries. Drizzle with more icing.

Note: Fresh raspberries in coulis can be replaced with Home-made Raspberry Jam (see page 193). Chopped or nibbed almonds can be added to the pastry for a nutty finish. Toasted caramelised flaked almonds can be shaped to sit on top, which gives a good crispy texture to contrast with the ice-cream. Lightly oil a baking tray. Scatter on to it 50 g of flaked almonds in 6 rough flat piles. Boil 60 g caster sugar and 2 tablespoons of water to a

golden caramel colour. Remove from the stove and leave to stand for 30 seconds. Spoon the caramel over each almond pile. Allow to set until crispy. The caramel should not totally cover the almonds; trickle over just enough to hold them together. Lift them off the tray and sit one on top of each Bakewell Tart Ice-cream for a stunning finish to this dish – or any other ice-cream or gâteau.

Iced Treacle Pudding

Serves 4

4 x 150 ml bowls

250 ml double cream
250 ml milk
250 g golden syrup
6 egg yolks

For the caramelised bananas
knob of butter
4 finger bananas *or* 2 large
    bananas
1 teaspoon Demerara sugar
6–8 teaspoons golden syrup, for
    trickling

To garnish
1 quantity Chocolate Sauce (see
    page 192)
clotted cream (optional)

This is a basic vanilla ice-cream recipe in which the sugar has been replaced by golden syrup. The results are richer than ever, especially with extra golden syrup trickling over the ice and a warm chocolate sauce to go with it. And don't be tempted to skip the caramelised bananas: golden syrup and bananas = tasty!

Bring the cream and milk to the boil. Whisk the egg yolks with the golden syrup, then pour on the boiled cream and whisk in well. Cook in a bowl over a pan of simmering water until the custard coats the back of a spoon. Leave to cool. Then churn in an ice-cream machine for 20–25 minutes, until thickened and increased in volume. Divide between the 4 moulds and leave in the freezer until set.

To caramelise the bananas, heat a frying pan with the knob of butter. Split the finger bananas lengthways, giving 2 pieces per portion. The large bananas can be cut at an angle, giving 2–3 thick slices per portion. Sit the bananas in the pan, and cook for 1–2 minutes, until they colour a little, before adding the Demerara sugar, which will begin to caramelise around the fruit. Add 1 tablespoon of cold water and the sugar will dissolve quickly, to cover all the banana pieces. Remove from the heat.

Dip the ice-cream moulds in hot water and turn out the 'sponge puddings'. Trickle golden syrup on top of each, and place a scroll of clotted cream next to the 'sponge', then the bananas. Serve the warm chocolate sauce separately.

Note: The banana slices can be caramelised by sprinkling with Demerara sugar on the flat side and cooked under the grill.

White and Dark Chocolate Coffee Bean Bombe

The coffee beans are the chocolate-coated variety, which can be bought from most good delicatessens, supermarkets and chocolate shops. They are not essential, but are exciting to bite into, releasing a good bitter coffee flavour that contrasts with the surrounding sweetness of the ice-cream. The Bailey's gives the parfait an extra edge. The bombe is best made 24 hours in advance.

Serves 6–8

1 x 1.2 l bombe mould/pudding bowl

For the white chocolate ice-cream
300 ml double cream
300 ml milk
7 egg yolks
150 g caster sugar
250 g grated white chocolate

For the dark chocolate parfait with coffee beans
2 egg yolks
25 g caster sugar
50 g dark chocolate, melted
150 ml double cream, lightly whipped
15 ml Bailey's (optional)
25 g chocolate-coated coffee beans (optional)

For the white chocolate ice-cream, bring to the boil the cream and the milk. Whisk the eggs and caster sugar until they form ribbons. Pour the cream on to the egg mixture and whisk together. Cook, in a bowl over a pan of simmering water, until it coats the back of a spoon. Add the grated white chocolate and stir in until the chocolate has melted. Pass through a sieve and allow to cool. Churn the mix in an ice-cream machine until it has thickened and increased in volume. Pour it into a container and allow to set a little firmer in the freezer, so it will be easier to work with. Use it to line the mould, leaving 150–300 ml domed hollow in the centre. Refreeze.

For the dark chocolate parfait, whisk the egg yolks and sugar together until they form ribbons. Stir in the melted chocolate along with the Bailey's. Once at room temperature, fold in the whipped cream and add the coffee beans. Pour the mix into the bombe and refreeze for several hours.

To serve, turn the bombe on to a decorative plate. You could pipe melted dark chocolate over it or top it with lots of chocolate pencils or shavings (see page 198). The Chocolate and Coffee Sauce on page 192 goes very well with this dish or, indeed, the Bitter Chocolate Sauce (see page 192).

Note: Chocolate chips or chocolate mint chips can be used in place of coffee beans. The white chocolate ice-cream can be made on its own and will fill a 900 ml bowl.

Summer Pudding Bombe

The explosive flavour of this bombe, balanced with the lighter vanilla parfait filling, justifies its name! It also looks wonderful with fresh summer berries in coulis just falling off it. This is probably best made 24 hours in advance. The Summer Pudding Ice-cream can be made on its own and will fill a 900 ml mould.

Defrost the berries and purée in a food-processor. Bring to the boil the cream with the milk. Whisk together the egg yolks and sugar until they form ribbons. Pour on the cream mixture and the puréed berries and whisk again. Cook in a bowl over a pan of simmering water until the mixture coats the back of a spoon. Add the liqueurs, if using, and strain the mixture through a sieve. Leave to cool.

Now churn it in an ice-cream maker for 20–25 minutes, until it has thickened and increased in volume. Before spooning it into the mould it's best to set it a touch firmer in the freezer when it will be easier to handle. Once it feels firm enough to use, spoon it into the mould. Push it around the sides, leaving a domed 150–300 ml hollow in the centre (or fill in the usual way if not making the parfait). Freeze. Once firm, the domed empty centre can be made smoother with a warmed dessertspoon.

To make the parfait, whisk the egg yolks, caster sugar and vanilla seeds to ribbon stage in a bowl over simmering water. Then take the bowl off the pan and continue to whisk until the mixture is at room temperature. Fold in the whipped cream and spoon into the hollowed Summer Pudding Bombe. Smooth over and refreeze for several hours until set.

Serve the bombe with coulis, made with frozen red summer berries (see page 190). This is a strong coulis, so a straight raspberry coulis can be used with a dash of crème de cassis, or crème de framboises to bind the fruit garnish. The quantity of garnish is up to you. Use whichever fruit you like – strawberries; raspberries; blackberries; blackcurrants; red and white currants; tayberries *or* bilberries.

I also like to either offer a spoon of Chantilly Cream (see page 185), clotted or pouring cream, Tuile biscuits (see page 178) or Caramelised Melba Toasts (see page 13), which represent the bread from the classic Summer Pudding!

Serves 6–8

1 x 1.2 l bombe mould/pudding bowl, if including the parfait, *or* 1 x 900 ml mould

For the Summer Pudding Ice-cream
500 g frozen mixed summer berries
250 ml double or whipping cream
75 ml milk
200 g caster sugar
6 egg yolks
65 ml crème de cassis (optional)
65 ml crème de framboise (optional)

For the vanilla parfait (optional)
50 g caster sugar
2 egg yolks
150 ml double cream, whipped to soft peaks
1 vanilla pod, split and seeds scraped out

fresh fruit to garnish (see below)

Note: Summer Pudding Bombe can be made in individual moulds: use 6 x 150 ml pudding basins.

Soufflés

Desserts we all seem a little afraid of! Perhaps it's because they don't carry a 'rising' guarantee? However, if you make sure the timing is right and the cooking just perfect then they come more than rubber-stamped.

Follow these golden rules.

1. The bowl and whisk must be scrupulously clean before you start working the egg whites and sugar.

2. One-third of the whisked whites must be mixed in with the base before you lightly fold in the rest.

3. The soufflé case/dish must be buttered and sugared right up to and including the top of the rim. If you do this the soufflé will not stick.

Unless otherwise stated, the soufflés featured here are to fill 4 x size 1 ramekins. Classic individual soufflé dishes are 10 cm diameter by 6 cm deep. If you use these, the quantities I have given will have to be doubled.

Ready-made custard can be used as an alternative to the pastry cream. Add 2 egg yolks to the custard for a stronger base.

Almost any flavour can be added to the vanilla base: chocolate, coffee, mint, strawberry, raspberry, apple, rhubarb, gooseberry, hazelnut, cherry kirsch, lemon, orange, passionfruit, exotic fruit, pears, etc.

You probably don't need me to tell you that the minute you get your soufflés out of the oven, put them on the table and eat them!

Vanilla Soufflé

Serves 4

4 x size 1 ramekins

8 tablespoons Pastry Cream (see page 184)
4 tablespoons caster sugar
4 egg whites
butter and caster sugar for lining ramekins
icing sugar for dusting

This recipe gives a base for all the soufflés but the vanilla flavour, which we often think of as 'plain', is sublime, especially if you use vanilla pods with the black seed spread throughout.

The secret of a good soufflé is to make sure that the centre remains soft and creamy. If you overcook it, the egg flavour will dominate anything else.

Preheat the oven to 200°C/400°F/Gas Mark 6.

Butter the ramekins well; then put a tablespoon of caster sugar into one. Turn the ramekin until the butter is coated, then tip the sugar into the next. Repeat until all the ramekins are lined. As the quantities given here will probably overfill the moulds, you could roll and tie a strip of greaseproof or parchment paper twice round the outside, and standing 3–5 cm above, the ramekin rim, before you line it with the butter and sugar, making sure to coat the paper too. This guarantees a risen soufflé and can be applied to any size of soufflé dish.

Whisk the egg whites in an electric mixer or by hand until half risen. Add the caster sugar and continue to whisk until they form soft peaks. Whisk a third of this 'meringue' mix into the pastry cream to loosen it. Now fold in the rest. Divide it between each mould.

If the mould has been wrapped in paper and the mix has overfilled, nothing else will need to be done. If just filling the mould, then smooth over the mix with a palette knife and slightly release the soufflé mix around the border with the tip of a small sharp knife.

Bake the soufflés for 10–12 minutes, until they are just firming and golden brown. Remove from the oven, carefully unwrap if papered, and dust with icing sugar before serving.

The vanilla soufflé goes well with many other flavours, but why not stay with the theme and try it with Vanilla Sauce Anglaise (see page 191) and Vanilla Ice-cream (see page 84). Or try Hot Chocolate Sauce (see page 192) or a fruit-flavoured coulis (see page 190). The quantity here will give you 4 nice-sized soufflés, but if you spoon the mix into 3 papered ramekins, you will have wonderful skyscraper soufflés.

Variations

Chocolate Soufflé

Warm the pastry cream lightly in the microwave or in a bowl over simmering water. Then whisk in the cocoa. Continue as for Vanilla Soufflé. Delicious with the Bitter Chocolate Sauce on page 192 or with fresh double cream. Grated chocolate can be added to the cocoa pastry-cream base before folding in the egg whites.

1 quantity vanilla base (see page 110)
25 g cocoa powder
50–100 g plain chocolate, grated (optional)

Lemon Soufflé

Add the zest and juice to the pastry-cream base and continue as for the Vanilla Soufflé. The Mint Ice-cream on page 86 is a great accompaniment, or try a Lemon Custard (see page 191).

1 quantity vanilla base (see page 110)
finely grated zest and juice of 2 lemons

Fruit-based Soufflés

These also use the Vanilla Soufflé base (see page 110) but halve the quantity of pastry cream and replace with the same amount of fruit purée or jam (see page 193) to flavour. You could also put in a splash of the appropriate fruit liqueur.

Whichever fruit – damson, plum, raspberry etc. – you use, you could chop a little, mix it with some coulis and spoon it into the ramekin base, then cover it with the soufflé mix. A rich fruit coulis or ice-cream will complete the dish.

Souffléd Vanilla Pancakes with Lemon and Vanilla Syrup

Cooking soufflés inside pancakes makes an exciting change. It also means you're going to eat the soufflé and what it's cooked in. The pancakes give a completely different feel and texture to the dish. You can fill them with any flavoured soufflé mix (the rich chocolate one is fabulous – see page 111) and even more so if you replace 15 g of the flour in the pancake batter (or 25 g for a really strong chocolate flavour!) with cocoa powder.

Have ready 12 squares of greaseproof paper for stacking.

Sift the flour and salt together. Beat the egg and milk into the flour. Stir in the melted butter. Now strain the batter through a sieve.

Heat a 15 cm pancake pan and trickle in a little oil. Add a thin layer of the batter to the pan. Cook on a medium heat for 30–40 seconds until golden. Turn the pancake over and continue to cook for a further 20–30 seconds. Remove it from the pan and place on greaseproof paper. Repeat the same process, stacking the pancakes between pieces of the paper. Leave to cool.

Reduce the Lemon and Vanilla Syrup by half until it is of a good thick coating consistency. Keep warm. This can be made in advance and reheated when needed.

Preheat the oven to 200°C/400°F/Gas Mark 6. Lay the pancakes on a large baking tray (two may be needed) lined with greaseproof paper. Spoon two dessertspoons of soufflé mix on to each pancake, placing the mix slightly to the front. Carefully fold over the pancake and leave it sitting lightly on top of the soufflé mix.

Bake for 5–6 minutes. The soufflé will now have risen and have kept a soft, creamy consistency in the centre. With a spatula or palette knife, lift the soufflés on to warmed plates. Dust with icing sugar and trickle with the syrup.

The pancakes are great on their own, but go well with thick cream or ice-cream.

Makes 12 x 15 cm pancakes
(2 per portion)

For the pancakes
100 g plain flour
pinch of salt
1 egg
300 ml milk
25 g butter, melted
vegetable oil for cooking

1 quantity Vanilla Soufflé base
(see page 110)
1 quantity Lemon and Vanilla
Syrup (see page 140)

Pecan Pie Soufflé

Serves 4

4 x 7.5 cm x 5 cm pastry rings, greased *or* 4 x size 1 ramekins, buttered and sugared

For the pastry cases
300 g sweet shortcrust pastry (see page 180)
50 g pecan nuts

For the souffleés
3 tablespoons condensed milk toffee (see page 187)
3 tablespoons pastry cream (see page 184)
4 egg whites
4 tablespoons caster sugar

For the toffee base
2 tablespoons condensed milk toffee (see page 187)
50 g chopped pecan nuts

For decorating
icing sugar, for dusting
1 quantity Bitter Chocolate Sauce (see page 192)

Pecan nuts are mainly grown in the USA – hence the long history of pecan pie. Pecan pie is a toffee-flavoured tart, made with golden or maple syrup or honey. This soufflé reproduces these flavours – from condensed milk toffee! Chocolate is another flavour that is often added to pecan pie. With this recipe, the chocolate is in the sauce.

Preheat the oven to 200°C/400°F/Gas Mark 6.

First make the pastry. Roast the pecan nuts in a medium oven for up to 10 minutes to enrich their flavour. Leave to cool. Grind them in a food-processor, and work them into the pastry along with the sugar.

Roll the pastry and use it to line the rings. Sit them on a baking tray, line them with greaseproof paper and baking beans or rice. Leave to rest for 20 minutes, then bake for 15–20 minutes until crisp. Remove from the oven and take out the greaseproof paper and baking beans. Do not switch off the oven. Allow the cases to cool, then remove them from the rings.

All pastry cases are delicate, so it's important now to handle them carefully! Roll strips of parchment paper around each pastry case twice to stand 3–5 cm above the rim. Tie gently. Butter the pastry cases all over, then dust them with caster sugar.

Make the toffee base: mix the chopped pecans with the toffee and divide it between the cases.

Now for the soufflé mix: whisk together the toffee and pastry cream. Whisk the egg whites until half risen, then add the caster sugar and continue to whisk to soft peaks. Take a third of the egg whites and whisk into the toffee pastry-cream base. Fold in the remainder gently. Spoon the mix into all the cases, filling them to above the edge of the pastry. Bake for 10–12 minutes until just firming and golden. Remove from the oven and dust with icing sugar. You could sit an extra pecan nut on top of each soufflé as a garnish. Serve the Bitter Chocolate Sauce separately.

Apple Strudel Soufflé

The story goes that the very thin pastry (filo) used to make strudel was originally from Turkey. This idea was passed on to the Austrians and Hungarians and the spicy apple-filled classic was born. It's often called Austrian, Bavarian or Hungarian, I always refer to it as tasty! Basically Apple Strudel is made from a mixture of chopped apples, almonds and currants flavoured with cinnamon and brandy.

A twist on the classic Apple Strudel! The filo pastry is used as a cup base, which is filled with spicy apples and topped with a light apple soufflé. Once baked and risen, you have the lightest apple strudel ever made!

Preheat the oven to 200°C/400°F/Gas Mark 6.

Lay two sheets of filo pastry on the work surface. Brush each slice with melted butter and sprinkle with Demerara sugar. Sit a second sheet of pastry on top of each and repeat the same process, and again with the last sheets. Cut each directly through the middle, giving you four halves. Sit a ring in the centre of one of the sheets and cut a circle around it, big enough to fill the ring to the top. Cut the remaining three circles. Grease the metal rings well and sit the filo discs in each one, pushing the pastry all around the sides to create a cup. Trim away any excess. Put the lined moulds on a parchment-papered baking tray. Line each pastry cup with greaseproof paper and baking beans, then bake for approximately 10–15 minutes until golden brown. Remove from the oven. Allow to cool a little before removing the beans and rings from the cups. These filo pastry 'ramekin' cups can now be placed on a wire rack to cool. Do not switch off the oven.

If you prefer, you can make 'biscuits' of the filo pastry and serve them with the soufflés made in ramekins rather than in the pastry cases. Follow all the instructions above and once the sheets are sandwiched cut them into the shape of your choice – fingers, triangles or discs. Bake on a parchment-papered tray for 10–15 minutes, until crispy and golden.

Now make the chunky apple and the purée. Chop the apples into a rough 5 mm dice, and cook with the sugar, lemon and cinnamon over a medium heat to a thick chunky purée. Blitz half to a smooth purée. Add the sultanas and raisins to the chunky half.

Serves 4

4 x 7.5 cm x 5 cm metal rings *or*
 4 x size 1 ramekins

For the cases
6 sheets filo pastry (see page
 183) *or* bought
25 g melted butter
Demerara sugar, for sprinkling

*For the chunky and smooth
 purée*
2 large Bramley apples, peeled
 and cored
75 g sugar
juice of ½ lemon
pinch of cinnamon
25 g mixed sultanas and raisins

For the soufflé
4 tablespoons tinned custard
6 tablespoons apple purée
2 egg whites
3 tablespoons caster sugar
extra caster sugar for lining
 cases

For the garnishes (optional)
1 quantity Sauce Anglaise (see
 page 191)
Calvados
icing sugar
cinnamon

Now for the soufflés. Whether using the filo cases or ramekins, it's best to cut strips of greaseproof or parchment paper and roll them around the moulds carefully – allowing 3 cm above each. Tie *gently* with string, particularly if using the filos, as they are very delicate. Next, carefully brush the insides of the cases and paper, fairly liberally, with melted butter, making sure all is covered. Spoon some caster sugar into one, roll the case around, carefully, covering the complete inside of the pastry or ramekin and the paper. Tip the sugar into the next and repeat with the other cases. Then sit them on a baking sheet. Spoon a heaped tablespoon of the chunky apple and fruit mix into the base of each.

Make the soufflé mix. Stir together the tinned custard with the smooth apple purée. Whisk the egg whites with the caster sugar in a clean bowl to a meringue with soft but firming peaks. Then fold it carefully into the apple custard and divide between the soufflé moulds. Bake for 10–12 minutes, until just firming and golden brown.

Take the soufflés from the oven and snip away the string. The paper will now unwrap from the moulds, leaving you with four well-risen Apple Strudel Soufflés. Dust with icing sugar and cinnamon before serving. Sauce Anglaise flavoured with Calvados is the perfect accompaniment.

Note: You can replace the homemade apple purée with jars of bought chunky and smooth, and use the rest of the tinned custard instead of making Sauce Anglaise. You now have the simplest of recipes to put together with an amazing homemade result.

'Brand' New Biscuits

A trio of dunking delights that all come from brand names – the Jaffa Cake, the Bourbon, and the Fig Roll. All three have been favourites since I was a child, hence the idea and the results. There's work involved in producing all three, but a platter featuring them is always a huge success! They are a great alternative to scones at tea-time or offer them as petits fours with a difference. They can even become a complete dessert, a Great British Pudding Plate, served with an Orange Custard (see page 191), for the Jaffa Cake, Chocolate and Coffee Sauce (see page 192) with the Bourbon and a nice scroll of Sticky Toffee Pudding Ice-cream (see page 101) with the Fig Roll.

Of course, you don't have to make all three, but please promise me you'll at least try one. Happy dunking!

Bourbon Biscuits

Serves 8

For the chocolate biscuits
150 g butter
150 g caster sugar, and extra for sprinkling
300 g self-raising flour
pinch of salt
8 tablespoons cocoa powder
1 egg beaten
8–10 teaspoons milk

For the brownies
225 g butter
150 g cocoa powder
4 eggs
450 g caster sugar
150 g plain flour
2 teaspoons vanilla essence
2 tablespoons strong coffee

For the ganache
225 g plain chocolate
250 ml double cream
2 egg yolks
25 g caster sugar

Note: Remember, these can be made in an individual pudding size, 10 x 5 cm, and served with Chocolate and Coffee Custard (see page 191).

Not the same as the ones you buy, but I've taken the idea and turned them into something that's even more exciting! And I do mean exciting! There's crisp biscuit, crumbling through moist brownie and creamy chocolate ganache. You can make them larger, 10 x 5 cm, and build them as a complete dessert.

Preheat the oven to 180°C/350°F/Gas Mark 4.

Make the biscuits first. Cream the butter and caster sugar. Sieve together the flour, salt and cocoa powder. Add the beaten egg to the creamed butter and then beat in the flour and cocoa mixture. Soften with the milk to a pastry dough consistency. Wrap the dough in clingfilm and refrigerate for 20 minutes. Roll the biscuit paste on a lightly floured surface to 3 mm thickness. Cut into 48 biscuits (or as many as possible) 6 x 3 cm (see Note below) and transfer to greaseproof-paper-lined baking trays. Make 8–10 holes, using a cocktail stick in the top of each and bake for 8–10 minutes. Take out, and while still warm, sprinkle with caster sugar. Leave to cool. Do not switch off the oven.

For the brownies, melt the butter and mix it with the cocoa powder. Whisk together the eggs and sugar and stir into the cocoa mixture. Mix in the remaining ingredients and spread the batter 5 mm thick into a shallow greaseproof-paper-lined baking tray. Bake for 6–7 minutes. Remove from the oven and leave to cool. Then cut into slightly smaller rectangles than the biscuits. The texture will be very moist.

Make the ganache filling. Melt the chocolate with half the cream in a bowl over simmering water. Whisk together the egg yolks and sugar until they form thick, creamy ribbons. Lightly whip the remaining cream. Mix the egg with the melted chocolate. Fold in the whipped cream and cool to a piping consistency.

To assemble the biscuits, turn over half of the biscuits and spread very thinly with ganache. Sit a brownie on top (the ganache will hold it in place). Using a small plain tube, pipe on some ganache. Place another rectangle of brownie on top. Spread a little ganache on another biscuit and stick it on top of the brownie. Your Bourbons are now ready.

Fig Rolls

This is not quite the classic biscuit! Here the fig purée still runs through the centre but there are two different biscuit pastes to wrap it in. One is flavoured with ground almonds while the second contains soft brown sugar, two different textures resulting in double the pleasure.

Place the figs in a saucepan with the water, bring to a simmer and cook for 10 minutes. Add the sugar and continue to cook until the liquid has almost evaporated. Purée the mix and allow it to cool. Then stir in the sponge-finger crumbs. Roll it into a log 30 cm long. To make handling easier, cut into two 15 cm pieces.

Make the second dough first. This is the outside dough and it needs to chill for 30 minutes before use. Rub together the flour, baking powder, sugar and butter to a breadcrumb texture. Add the egg and mix to a dough. Wrap it in clingfilm and chill for 30 minutes.

Now make the first dough. Mix together the ground almonds and the sugars. Beat an egg and add it with the lemon juice to the almond mix and work to a firm paste. Dust the work surface with icing sugar and roll the paste 30 cm long and wide enough to roll round the fig log. Beat the remaining egg and brush the paste. Cut into two 15-cm pieces. Place the fig logs on top of each and roll. Chill.

Preheat the oven to 180°C/350°F/Gas Mark 4. Lightly flour the work surface and roll the second dough to 30 cm long and wide enough to cover the first dough. Again, cut it into two 15 cm pieces. Brush with the remaining egg and sit the wrapped fig roll on top. Cover with the dough. Press the rolls slightly to take on the classic shape, then cut, making 7–8 biscuits from each. Press a fork on top of each and draw it across to create a channel effect. Refrigerate for 15–20 minutes. Leave them plain or brush with milk and sprinkle with caster sugar. Bake for 20–25 minutes. Remove from the oven and cool on wire racks.

Makes approximately 15 biscuits

For the filling
200 g ready-to-eat dried figs
150 ml water
50 g dark soft brown sugar
50 g dry sponge fingers, crushed
   or crumbled

For the second dough
250 g plain flour
¾ teaspoon baking powder
90 g light soft brown sugar
125 g butter
1 egg
1 tablespoon milk (optional)
3 teaspoons caster sugar
   (optional)

For the first dough
375 g ground almonds
185 g caster sugar
185 g icing sugar
2 teaspoons lemon juice
2 eggs

Jaffa Cake Pudding

Serves 6–8

1 baking tray, cake tin *or*
  Yorkshire pudding mould,
  lined with clingfilm

For the jelly
1 x 11 g sachet powdered
  gelatine
300 ml fresh orange juice
  (approximately 4–5 oranges)
finely grated zest from all the
  oranges
75 g caster sugar

For the sponge base
3 eggs
75 g caster sugar
75 g plain flour
finely grated zest of 1 orange
40 g unsalted butter, melted

For the orange syrup
grated zest and juice of 1 orange
2 tablespoons water
50 g caster sugar

For the ganache
300 ml double cream
2 tablespoons Cointreau *or*
  Grand Marnier (optional)
250 g good-quality plain
  chocolate
finely grated zest of 1 orange
2 egg yolks
25 g caster sugar

As a youngster I loved Jaffa Cake biscuits (still do!). Biting through the chocolate into the tangy orange jelly then the soft sponge. Yum!

This recipe has three main components and consequently looks quite awesome when it's finished! It does take time but the results are just immense. And I've included a recipe for Quick Jaffa Cake Pudding, so there's no excuse for not trying one or the other.

If you're taking on the main recipe, here are some points to remember. There are three stages: the sponge base; the orange jelly; the chocolate topping. It's important to make the orange jelly first, of course, a few or even 24 hours in advance. You can substitute bought fresh orange juice for the freshly squeezed I suggest. The addition of finely grated zest from one or two oranges to bought juice will increase the flavour.

The sponge is a basic sponge recipe with the addition of orange zest to help carry and spread the rich orange taste, but you can use a bought sponge base instead.

When making the ganache, you can leave out the egg yolk and sugar mixture and simply fold in the whipped cream.

I like to serve an orange-flavoured Sauce Anglaise, page 191, with this pudding but fresh cream goes well too.

To make the jelly, dissolve the gelatine in a little hot water. Bring the orange juice to the boil with the zest and caster sugar, then simmer for 2 minutes. Remove from the heat, add the gelatine and once completely dissolved strain the syrup through a sieve to remove the zest: this prevents the jelly from becoming too bitter and strong. Now pour a tablespoon of the mix onto a saucer and chill. If the jelly sets firm once it is cold, the mix is ready; if it seems a little too soft, add a little more dissolved gelatine. Pour the jelly into the lined cake tin or tray so that it is 1 cm thick and leave it in the fridge to set. Cut out 6 to 8 x 6-cm jelly discs. Freeze any leftover jelly to use another time.

Preheat the oven to 190°C/375°F/Gas Mark 5. To make the sponge, whisk the eggs and sugar together in a bowl over a pan of hot water until light, creamy and at least doubled in volume. Remove from the heat and continue to whisk until cold. Gently fold in the flour, orange zest and melted butter. Pour it into the moulds so that they are three-quarters full, and bake for 15–20 minutes. If you are using one large mould, cook for 25–30 minutes. Remove from the oven and leave to cool.

Now cut out discs from the centre of each cake to make space for the jelly: take a 6 cm diameter cutter and press into the sponge 1 cm deep, leaving a 5 mm border and a 5 mm thick base. (If you are making a large Jaffa Cake, cut out a disc of sponge 2 cm deep, leaving a 1 cm border and base. The sponge will lift out, leaving space for the jelly.) *Do not cut through the base.*

To make the rich orange syrup for soaking the sponge, mix the orange zest and juice, the water and sugar in a pan. Bring to a simmer and cook for 1–2 minutes. Pour 1 tablespoon of syrup over each sponge base and place the jelly discs into the sponge bases.

Now for the chocolate ganache filling. Melt together half the cream, the Cointreau or Grand Marnier, the chocolate and the orange zest. Whisk the egg yolks and sugar together until the mixture trails off the whisk in ribbons. Lightly whip the remaining cream. Stir the egg and sugar mix into the chocolate, then gently fold in the whipped cream. Leave it to cool, stirring occasionally until it has reached piping consistency. Pipe or spoon the chocolate ganache over the jelly, 1 cm thick. Ripple it with a palette knife for that 'Jaffa' effect.

Last, make the shiny topping. Melt the chocolate with the cream, stir in the softened butter, spoon a thin layer on top of the puddings and chill.

This pudding is best eaten at room temperature. To serve, remove the puddings from the moulds and for a really shiny finish place them under the grill for a few seconds or fire with a gas gun (see page 11).

For the shiny topping
100 g good-quality plain chocolate
120 ml double cream
25 g unsalted butter, softened

'Brand' Jaffa Cake Biscuits

Small tartlet cases 6 x 1 cm can be used to make biscuit-like Jaffa cakes. Follow the complete recipe. Fill the tartlet cases (approximately 24) with the sponge mix and bake for 10 minutes. Cut the jelly smaller to match, and pipe the ganache a little less thick. It's important to finish the cakes with the extra shiny topping.

Quick Jaffa Cake Pudding

Serves 8–10

1 x 23 cm round, shallow cake tin
 or dish, lined with clingfilm

1 x packet of orange jelly, cut
 into cubes
375 ml orange juice
275 g plain chocolate, broken
 into pieces
350 ml double cream
1 x 25 cm bought sponge *or* flan
 case

For the shiny topping
175–225 g plain chocolate,
 broken into pieces
50 g butter

This is easy to make and results in a wonderful family Jaffa Cake.

The ganache is much simpler than the version in the main recipe and is the only part of the dish you have to make from scratch yourself. The shiny topping is an optional extra, but gives the dish a really classy edge.

Put the orange jelly pieces into a jug or bowl. Bring 150 ml of the orange juice to the boil and pour on top of the jelly. Stir until the jelly has dissolved then add the rest of the juice. Pour into a tin or dish. Chill until set. The jelly should be 1–2 cm thick.

For the chocolate ganache topping, put the broken chocolate and half of the cream into a bowl and place it over a pan of simmering water until the chocolate has melted. Remove and leave to cool. Whip the rest of the cream to soft peaks and fold it into the cooled melted chocolate. Chill for a few minutes to a smooth spreading consistency, but do not let it set.

Turn the jelly out of the tin and remove the clingfilm. Lay the jelly in the flan case and spread the chocolate mix on top to give a domed finish. Ripple it with a palette knife.

Leave in the refrigerator for 30 minutes to set. The Quick Jaffa Pudding is now ready to serve or to be finished with the shiny chocolate glaze.

Melt the chocolate and the butter together in a bowl over warm water. Spoon or spread it carefully over the chocolate ganache.

Note: Once chilled the shiny topping will have a matt finish. To recreate the shine, pop under a hot grill for seconds or glaze with a gas gun (see page 11). The sponge base can be flavoured with a sprinkling of Cointreau or Grand Marnier. If you are not using the shiny topping, why not grate some chocolate over it instead?

Seville Orange Marmalade Jelly

You could make this from my homemade marmalade (see page 194), but a jar of good-quality marmalade will also do the trick. It's a sweet jelly, but with the delicious bitter bite of Seville oranges. Serve it with just a spoonful of extra thick cream or turn it into a totally different experience: the chocolate mousse served with the Pear Belle Hélène (see page 28–9) spooned next to it gives a delicious combination of orange and chocolate. Decorate the plates with sugar-glazed orange segments and fine chocolate pencils (see page 198).

Serves 6

6 x 150 ml plastic pudding bowls

100 g Seville orange marmalade
150 ml water
350 ml fresh orange juice, strained
100 g caster sugar
4 gelatine leaves

Bring the marmalade, water, orange juice and sugar to the boil. Meanwhile, soak the gelatine in cold water. Once it is soft, drain and squeeze it. Add the gelatine to the marmalade mix, stir until it has dissolved, then strain to remove any peel in the marmalade, or pour it straight into the moulds, leaving in the coarse bits. Allow to cool before refrigerating until set, 1–2 hours. To turn out the jellies, submerge the bowls in hot water to the rim, then take out and squeeze gently over the plates. The jelly will plop out ready to serve.

Note: One or two measures of Cointreau or Grand Marnier can be added to the mix for Adult Jellies!

Prune and Armagnac 'Black Cap' Rice Pudding

Black Cap Pudding is an old English steamed vanilla sponge topped with currants, hence the black cap. This dish has a similar appearance, but different flavours. Here the black cap is luscious prunes soaked in Armagnac, which is then made into a caramel to pour into the base of the dish. Rich rice pudding sits on top. When you turn it out – well, wait and see!

Preheat the oven to 180°C/350°F/Gas Mark 4.

Soak the prunes in the Armagnac for 20–30 minutes, then strain them, keeping the juices. Dissolve the sugar in three-quarters of the water, then bring to the boil for a few minutes without shaking the pan until the caramel is golden brown. Add the remaining water, Amagnac juices and reboil. Remove from the heat. Pour the caramel into the soufflé dishes, divide the prunes between them and leave the caramel to set.

Place the rice in a saucepan with some cold water, bring it to the boil, drain, and refresh under running cold water. In a saucepan, bring to the boil 450 ml of the milk, half the sugar and the butter, then add the rice. Reduce to a simmer and cook until the rice is tender (10–12 minutes). Beat together the egg yolks and remaining sugar. Bring to the boil the cream with the remaining milk and pour it on to the yolks, stirring all the time. Mix this with the rice, then pour carefully over the set caramel. Stand them in a roasting tray three-quarters filled with hot water and bake for 10–15 minutes. Remove from the roasting tray and allow to cool and set, then refrigerate.

To serve, dip the dishes in hot water and release them around the edges with a sharp knife. Turn the dishes over on to pudding plates or bowls.

The rich custard holds the rice pudding firmly together while the Armagnac and prune caramel sits on top and trickles down the dish.

Serves 4

4 x size 1 soufflé dishes

For the prunes and caramel
18–20 ready-to-eat stoned
   prunes, halved
3–4 tablespoons Armagnac
175 g caster sugar
250 ml water

For the rice pudding
600 ml milk
75 g caster sugar
25 g unsalted butter
100 g short grain rice
4 egg yolks
150 ml double cream

Golden Syrup Floating Islands with Crispy Pineapple

Floating Islands are meringues that have been poached in milk, as light as soufflés, a great contrast to the crispy pineapple. The golden syrup finishes the dish, drizzling over the Islands of Rhodes!

Whisk the egg whites to soft peaks. Then add 3 tablespoons of the caster sugar and continue to whisk to a good thick firm peak. If the meringue is not quite holding its shape, add the remaining tablespoon of sugar and continue to whisk. While the meringue is being whisked heat the milk, mixed with 300–600 ml of water. Shape the meringue between two tablespoons into quenelles (see page 11) or with an ice-cream scoop and lower it carefully into the milk. Alternatively spoon it into the milk with a large serving spoon. Poach for 12–15 minutes, turning the Islands over after the first 6–7 minutes.

Slice the pineapple into 8. Remove the core with a 2.5 cm diameter pastry cutter. Dust the pineapple rings with caster sugar on one side only, sit them on a greased baking tray and place under the grill. The sugar will slowly start to caramelise, leaving a crispy topping. Repeat for extra crispiness. Then sit them on plates, 2 per portion, and place a warm Floating Island in the centre of each. Trickle golden syrup over each Island.

Note: The Floating Islands can be served as a dish on their own with just a spoonful or two of warm Sauce Anglaise (see page 191). Flavour the milk with a few strips of peeled lemon rind before you cook the Islands, and a fresh vanilla pod, split, scraped and added to the meringue is delicious. The Bitter Chocolate Sauce on page 192 is a great accompaniment.

Serves 4

4 large egg whites
3–4 tablespoons caster sugar
600 ml milk

1 small–medium fresh pineapple, skinned
caster (*or* Demerara) sugar to glaze
golden syrup

Sabayon Glazed Summer Pudding

Serves 6

6 x size 1 ramekins *or* 6 large
  glasses *or* 6 glass bowls

For the summer pudding
1 punnet raspberries
1 punnet strawberries
1 punnet blackberries
3–4 tablespoons mixed
  redcurrants, blackcurrants and
  blueberries
25–50 g icing sugar
150 ml water *or* sweet white
  wine *or* champagne
12 slices thick sliced white bread

For the sabayon
3 egg yolks
60 g caster sugar
4 tablespoons casssis *or* crème
  de framboise
150 ml sweet white wine

The summer fruits are layered with the soaked bread in soufflé dishes or glasses and finished with a thick, creamy sabayon, which can be flavoured with cassis, crème de framboises or sweet white wine. A good sabayon should be really thick and almost hold its own with a spoon (or your finger!) run through it.

Wash all of the berries carefully and drain. Place them in a large saucepan with the water, wine or champagne, along with 25 g of the icing sugar. Bring to a simmer and cook for 5–6 minutes until the fruit is tender. The sugar and water or wine will have created a syrup. Taste for sweetness and, if a little bland and bitter, add the remaining sugar. Leave the fruit to cool in its juices.

Cut the bread into discs to fit the ramekins. Pour three-quarters of the syrup off the fruit and soak the bread slices in it. Then lay a slice in the base of each mould. Divide half of the fruit and remaining syrup between each portion. Lay another slice of bread on top and then the remaining fruit.

For the sabayon, whisk the egg yolks, caster sugar, liqueur or sweet white wine in a bowl over simmering water until thick, creamy and doubled in volume, then spoon over the top of each summer pudding. If using ramekins, you can give them a golden glazed finish: place under a hot grill until coloured.

Note: The summer pudding stage can be made up to 2–3 days in advance and refrigerated. Frozen summer fruits can be used and warmed with the sugar and sweet white wine or champagne.

Fried Apple Turnover Slice

*These must be the only Apple Turnovers that don't
have any puff pastry. They are, in fact, apple
sandwiches shallow-fried in a batter, but you can
put in more or less any sweet filling, including jam.
It can be a very quick pudding, with apple filling
from a jar, but here we'll use fresh.*

Cut the apples into rough 5 mm dice. Melt a small
knob of butter in a saucepan over a medium heat
and add the apples, cinnamon and sugar. Cook for
a few minutes until tender. Leave to cool. Butter the
slices of bread on one side only. Divide the apples
between 4 slices, sitting in small piles in the centre
of each slice. Sandwich the other slice on top,
pressing around for the two buttered sides to stick together. Cut off the
crusts, or use a large round pastry cutter to make circular sandwiches.
Whisk together the eggs, sugar and cream, then place the sandwiches in
the batter. Turn them over and leave them to soak for a few minutes.

Melt the butter in a large frying pan. Once it is bubbling, sit the sandwiches
in the pan and fry on a low heat until golden brown. Turn them carefully
and fry on the other side also to a golden brown. Take them out and eat at
once with a spoonful of extra thick cream or ice-cream.

Note: Another favourite 'sandwich' of mine is made with tinned peaches:
drain, dry lightly, and cut the fruit into 1 cm dice. Bind with a spoonful or
two of raspberry jam (see page 193), *or* bought jam, and continue as
above. Serve with vanilla ice-cream for a Fried Peach Melba Slice. Here
are a few more ideas for fillings: rhubarb with lemon curd; toasted
almonds or hazelnuts with the apple; cherry jam and chocolate;
pineapple and coconut.

Serves 4

For the sandwiches
2–3 Granny Smith apples, peeled
   and cored
butter
pinch of cinnamon
1 teaspoon caster *or* light soft
   brown sugar
8 slices medium white bread

For the batter
4 eggs
4 tablespoons caster sugar
4 tablespoons double cream
50 g butter

Hot Pear Puffs

Serves 6

6 whole pears
juice of ½ lemon
1 vanilla pod (optional)
450 ml water
350 g caster sugar
500 g puff pastry (see page
   181–2), *or* bought
2 egg yolks, lightly forked
150 g frangipane (see page 28, a
   quarter of this quantity will be
   enough)

With similar ingredients to a pear and almond flan, these puffs have a different texture and a sort of different taste. It's the balance of the two that changes the eating. These are whole poached pears, filled with a spoonful of frangipane, then wrapped in puff pastry. Cutting through the pastry to release the aromatic scent, and the flavour of almonds with pear is exquisite. Need I say more?

Peel the pears, leaving the stalks on. Sit them upright in a saucepan, sprinkle with the lemon juice, put in the vanilla pod (if using), the sugar and water. Bring the syrup to the boil and poach the pears for 8–10 minutes. They can now be left to cool in the syrup. (They will keep for up to 10 days if refrigerated in the syrup.) Alternatively, poach the pears in the liquor described on page 128.

Preheat the oven to 200°C/400°F/Gas Mark 6.

Remove the pears from the syrup and core carefully from the base with an apple corer. Leave the pears on a cloth to drain any excess syrup. Roll out the pastry into a long 60 x 18–20 cm rectangle and brush with the egg yolk. Trim the pastry for a straight edge, before cutting it into 6 long strips 2–2.5 cm thick. Fill each pear with frangipane and then wrap it in the pastry, egg wash side out, from the stalk to the base, overlapping the pastry as you go. Trim away any excess.

Stand the pears on a greased baking tray and refrigerate for 20–30 minutes to set the pastry. Bake for 20–30 minutes until a crispy golden brown. The pastry will have puffed, but kept the pear shape. Serve with Sauce Anglaise (see page 191), cream or ice-cream.

Note: Sauce Anglaise can be flavoured with Poire William to enhance the pear taste. The Toffee Cream (see page 187) also goes well. Perhaps add a tin of pears to the poaching syrup and purée, to make a pear sorbet. The iced sorbet with the Hot Pear Puffs is always a winner!

Trio of Rum Babas

Serves 5

15 x 4 cm x 5 cm dariole tins *or* 5
   x 150 ml pudding basins *or*
   6–8 x 7.5 cm savarin rings,
   greased

For the dough
20 g yeast
50 ml tepid milk
250 g plain flour
10 g sugar
pinch of salt
3 eggs, beaten
25 g butter, softened
50 g sultanas (optional)

For the lemon and vanilla syrup
100 ml stock syrup (see page
   188)
100 ml lemon juice
finely grated zest of ½ lemon
1 vanilla pod, split
50 g caster sugar

For the strawberry syrup
200 ml stock syrup (see page
   188)
4 tablespoons crème de fraise
   (optional)
1 tablespoon strawberry jam

For the mint syrup
200 ml stock syrup (see page
   188)
2 large stems fresh mint

The baba dough was invented by Stohrer, a Polish pastry chef. His idea was taken further when Auguste Julien invented the Savarin. He was one of three brothers who owned a patisserie in Paris during the nineteenth century and had worked with the famous French gastronome Brillat-Savarin. Savarin had given him his sweet syrup recipe, so Auguste named this dish in his honour. Classically, babas contain sultanas and are baked in darioles, while savarins are plain and cooked in ring moulds. This trio honours the three Parisian patissiers, for each baba has its own 'Savarin' flavoured syrup.

Preheat the oven to 200°C/400°F/Gas Mark 6.

Mix the yeast with the milk until it has dissolved. Sieve the flour, sugar and salt together into a mixing bowl. Add the yeast and milk to the flour mix and stir in. Then add the eggs and work to a smooth consistency with the sultanas. Pipe the dough into the greased darioles. Cover all with a warm cloth and allow to prove in a warm place for 15–20 minutes, remove the cloth if the dough begins to rise close to the top of the moulds. Bake for 10 minutes. Remove from the oven and allow to cool for 10 minutes before turning out.

To make the lemon and vanilla syrup, bring all the ingredients to the boil. Remove from the heat, reserve 4–5 tablespoons of the syrup, then sit 5 babas in the rest to absorb it.

For the strawberry syrup, bring all the ingredients to the boil and strain through a sieve. Reserve 4–5 tablespoons of the syrup and soak 5 babas in the rest.

For the mint syrup, proceed as for the other syrups, but leave the mint leaves to infuse, while soaking the babas. As before, keep 4–5 tablespoons separate before you soak the babas.

Boil the reserved syrups separately, until reduced by half. Remove the babas from the soaking syrup, and glaze with a little of their own thick, intensely flavoured syrup before serving.

To garnish, sit the Candied Syrup Lemon Strips or wedges (if using) next to the vanilla and lemon baba. Put a spoonful of loose strawberry jam (see page 193) across the top of the strawberry one, or finish with fresh strawberries. A small scroll of Mint Ice-cream complements the mint baba, with chocolate scrolls or a pencil to finish. These are ideas for you to play with.

Note: If you use the 150 ml pudding basins, serve one baba per portion. They will take 30 minutes to prove and 30–35 minutes to bake. Choose one syrup to soak the babas and treble the volume. If you use savarin rings prove and cook for the same time as the small darioles, then soak in syrup. If making savarins, a scoop or scroll of sorbet or ice-cream placed in the centre with fresh fruits looks beautiful and tastes as good as it looks.

For the garnishes (optional)
Candied Syrup Lemon Strips or sliced wedges (see page 188)
strawberry jam (see page 193)
1 quantity Mint Ice-cream (see page 86)
chocolate scrolls or pencils (see page 198)
sprigs of fresh mint

Warm Apple Soup with Crispy Apple Dumplings and Apple Cider Sorbet

Serves 6

For the apple and cider sorbet
700 g Granny Smith apples,
    peeled, cored and quartered
juice of 2 lemons
250 ml stock syrup (see page 188)
125 ml sweet apple cider

For the warm apple soup
200 ml water
160 ml apple juice
120 ml sweet cider
35 g caster sugar
5 ml lemon juice
2 apples, preferably Cox's,
    peeled, cored and quartered
1 cinnamon stick *or* pinch of
    ground cinnamon

For the crispy apple dumplings
6 egg-cups, greased
40 g shelled hazelnuts
1 Granny Smith apple, peeled
    and cored
3 dried apricots
10 g icing sugar, and extra for
    sprinkling
15 ml Frangelico *or* Amaretto
    liqueur (optional)
2 sheets filo pastry (see page
    183 *or* buy it)
1–2 teaspoons fresh white
    breadcrumbs

There are three components to this dish, but the apple soup and the sorbet can both stand on their own. But do try the complete dish: it gives you lots of different textures, consistencies and, of course, flavours – a stunning experience!

Make the sorbet: stew the apples with the lemon juice and a little of the syrup for 15–20 minutes until tender. Leave to cool, then blitz to a purée. Stir in the remaining syrup and cider, and churn in an ice-cream maker for 20–25 minutes. (If you do not have an ice-cream machine, you can still make the sorbet. See page 83 for freezing instructions.) Now freeze until the sorbet has completely set.

Make the soup: bring the water, apple juice, cider, sugar and lemon juice to the boil. Put in the apples and the cinnamon. Simmer for 15–20 minutes until the apples are tender. Remove from the heat, discard the cinnamon stick, and blend to a purée. Then, for a smoother finish, strain through a sieve. This is best made well in advance and can be served chilled, at room temperature or hot.

To make the dumplings, preheat the oven to 200°C/400°F/Gas Mark 6. Roast the hazelnuts for 6–8 minutes, then place them in a clean cloth and rub them together to remove the skins. Dice the apricot and apple into 5 mm pieces and mix together. Put the nuts in a food-processor or coffee grinder with the icing sugar. Add the liqueur and continue to blitz until smooth. Tip the paste into a bowl and mix the fruit into it.

Brush a sheet of filo pastry with butter, sprinkle it with some icing sugar and the breadcrumbs. Top with the second sheet of filo and cut into 6. Working quickly, to prevent the filo drying, carefully line each egg cup with the pastry, then fill with the apple mixture and fold over the edges of the pastry to enclose it. The egg cups can now be turned out to give you 6 domed dumplings. You can make them in advance and cook them when you need them (or even bake them beforehand and reheat in the microwave). Place the dumplings on a greased baking tray and bake for

approximately 12–14 minutes until they are golden.

To serve, pour the Apple Soup into bowls, and put in the dumplings – they will stand well above the soup. Shape the sorbet between two tablespoons into quenelles (see page 11) or scoop it into balls and sit it in the soup.

Note: It's not essential to shape the dumplings in egg cups: you can spoon the filling into the centre of the filo squares, then lift and twist to give you little money-bags.

If you wish to serve the soup hot, grate some fresh apple, or cut it into 'julienne' strips, bind it with a drop or two of lemon juice and put some in each bowl. It provides a base for the apple sorbet to sit on so that it does not melt too quickly in the soup.

Shred one or two mint leaves finely and add to the soup just before serving.

The Pear Plate

Serves 8

This dessert is totally devoted to pears. It's made up of 4 contrasting dishes, all in small portions, so that you get a taste of everything. The complete recipe serves 8. If you don't want to make all four dishes, choose the ones you'd prefer. All of them can be treated as complete dishes to stand on their own, but as you see on the previous page I have served them all together on one large plate – so exciting you just don't know where to start. If you keep to these quantities but use larger moulds, the individual recipes will serve 4. All can be made well in advance – the poached pears, the jelly and the sorbet. The pies can be pre-baked and warmed through when needed, or place them in the oven when you've either just started or finished your main course and 20 minutes later they will be ready.

Poach the pears first: this gives you the syrup for the jelly and the sorbet. The sabayon to glaze the pears can be made before you eat and then rewhisked before serving.

Glazed Poached Pears

375 ml sweet white wine, preferably Sauternes

125 ml orange juice

juice of 1 lemon

150 g caster sugar

2 whole cloves

4 pears, peeled, halved lengthways and cored

For the sabayon

4 egg yolks

125 ml pear poaching liquor

50 g caster sugar

Bring the wine, orange juice, lemon juice, caster sugar and cloves to the boil. Reduce to a simmer, add the pears and cook for 15 minutes until tender. Remove from the heat and leave the pears to cool in the syrup. Once cool, cut the pears in half to give you two quarters per portion. These can be kept and served cool, or warmed quickly in a drop of syrup in the pan or the microwave before serving. Reserve the rest of the syrup for the sorbet and/or the jelly.

To make the sabayon, whisk together all the ingredients in a bowl over a pan of simmering water, until doubled in volume, and of a thick coating consistency. It is now ready to spoon over the pears and glaze under the grill or with a gas gun (see page 11).

Note: A splash or two of Poire William liqueur can be added to the poaching liquid for extra zip.

Pear Sorbet

Place the pears and the liquor in a saucepan and simmer until the fruit is completely tender. Liquidise to a smooth purée and allow to cool. Then churn in an ice-cream machine for 20–25 minutes until it has thickened and increased in volume. Pour into a container and freeze. If an ice-cream machine is unavailable, then simply freeze and whisk from time to time (see page 83). Once frozen, blitz in a food-processor and refreeze for a smoother consistency.

The sorbet can be scooped and served directly on the plate, which should be dusted with a little icing sugar to prevent it sliding about, or in a tuile basket (see pages 178–9).

450 g pears, peeled, cored and chopped
150 ml pear poaching liquor (from the Glazed Pears)

Pear Jelly

Set these small jellies in egg cups for a domed shape or dariole moulds (as pictured); both look quite stunning. Or pour it 3–5 cm deep into a tray or dish and when it has set cut it into the shape of your choice.

250–300 ml pear poaching liquor (from the Glazed Pears)
1–2 leaves gelatine, soaked in water

This quantity of gelatine will give you a soft, delicate jelly. Add a leaf at a time, then pour a spoonful or two of the jelly onto a saucer. If it sets it contains enough gelatine. If not, add another leaf, and continue to test until the jelly will set.

Bring the syrup to the boil and add the soaked gelatine, stir until it has dissolved then strain through a fine sieve. Pour into the moulds and refrigerate until set. To turn out, dip the moulds in hot water and release the jelly on to the plates.

Pear Pies

8 x 5 cm x 1 cm tartlet cases *or* 1
 15 cm flan ring, buttered

250 g sweet shortcrust pastry
 (see page 180)
6 large pears, peeled, cored and
 diced
knob of butter
4 tablespoons caster sugar
granulated sugar for sprinkling

Line the tartlet cases with the pastry, and cut out 8 larger discs for the lids. Melt the butter, add the pears with the caster sugar and cook for a few minutes until you have a chunky purée. Remove from the heat and allow to cool. Fill the pastry cases with the pears, giving generous domed portions. Brush the edge of the pastry cases with egg yolk or water, sit the lids on top and seal the edges. Refrigerate before baking (they can be made well in advance) to allow the pastry to rest.

Preheat the oven to 180°C/350°F/Gas Mark 4. Brush each pie with milk and sprinkle with granulated sugar. Bake for 15–20 minutes until golden brown. A 15 cm tart will take 25–30 minutes. Serve with Sauce Anglaise (see page 191).

Fromage Frais and Strawberry Mille-Feuilles

Serves 4

750 g puff pastry *or* quick puff
 pastry (see page 181–2) *or*
 bought

For the mousse
625 ml fromage frais
50 g caster sugar
1 vanilla pod, split
3 leaves gelatine, soaked in water
 until softened then drained
150 ml whipped double cream

Translated mille-feuilles means a thousand leaves, and the leaves are the thin crispy layers that result from the rising of the puff pastry. Mille-feuilles take on all sorts of faces but perhaps the one we all recognise is the jam, cream and iced-top variety, available from most bakers. This version isn't moving too far from that, but it's a lot lighter and healthier to eat: here we are building a thousand leaves of crispiness with a light vanilla fromage frais mousse (see page 149), finished with fresh strawberries.

Preheat the oven to 200°C/400°F/Gas Mark 6.

Line two baking trays with greaseproof paper. Roll the puff pastry on a floured work surface, 2–3 mm thick. Cut 12 rectangles 11 x 6 cm and lay them on parchment-papered baking trays. Leave to rest for 15 minutes, then bake for 20 minutes. Reduce the oven temperature to 130°C/260°F/Gas Mark ½ and continue to cook for a further 10–15 minutes. The mille-feuilles will now be crispy and golden.

Make the mousse. Place the fromage frais, caster sugar and split vanilla pod in a saucepan and bring to a simmer. Remove from the heat, add the gelatine leaves and stir until they have dissolved. Strain and leave to cool and chill, stirring occasionally to a creamy consistency. Once chilled and beginning to thicken, fold in the whipped cream. Chill again for the mousse to set.

If you are using the fresh strawberries alone, leave them as they are. Otherwise bind them with the strawberry coulis.

To build the mille-feuilles, lay a pastry rectangle on each of the plates. Spoon some mousse on top, then either some of the strawberries or trickle over a tablespoon of strawberry jam or coulis (or vice versa). Top with another pastry, and repeat. The third pastry can be dusted with icing sugar or left natural. A thousand leaves have grown. Any mousse left over can be served separately with summer fruits or on its own.

Note: Sprinkle some lemon 'parmesan' (see page 28) around the plate for a pretty effect and extra flavour – the bitter-sweet lemon works well with the mousse and the strawberries. Sit a 5 cm diameter disc cutter covered with clingfilm on the top pastry and dust the icing sugar around it to give a golden disc centre. Put a whole fresh strawberry in the circle. Alternatively, cut a 5 cm disc template and dust inside the disc, place the strawberry on the sugar. The whole strawberries can also be dipped in caramel to give a cracked sugar glaze: boil some sugar and water together until golden brown, then dip the strawberries, on cocktail sticks into it, and leave on oiled paper to dry – toffee strawberries.

For the strawberries
225–350 g fresh strawberries, washed and halved
150–250 ml strawberry coulis (see page 190) (optional) *or* 8 tablespoons of strawberry jam (see page 193)

149

Warm Black Forest Gâteau

Serves 6

6 x 8 cm x 6 cm rings and a
    baking sheet *or* 6 ovenproof
    pudding basins, buttered

For the gâteaux
175 g plain chocolate, chopped
175 g butter, unsalted and
    chopped
4 whole eggs
4 egg yolks
75 g caster sugar
75 g plain flour

For the cherry compôte
200 g fresh black cherries
50 ml stock syrup (see page 188)
kirsch (optional)
3–4 tablespoons black cherry
    jam

1 quantity vanilla ice-cream (see
    page 84) *or* bought
clotted cream

The most exciting part of this dish is cutting into the gâteau and seeing the warm gooey chocolate ooze from the centre. The rich moist chocolate mixed with the black cherry compôte is just a dream to eat. A whole new take on a very old formula.

To enjoy that warm gooey centre it has to be baked to order. You can leave the mix in the moulds in the fridge, ready to be popped into the oven. They only take minutes to bake, so you won't have to wait long for your pudding. Use rings rather than bowls if you can to cook them: you can lift off the rings to show off the whole puddings, as featured on page 151, if you don't have the rings, the puddings will have to stay in the bowls.

Preheat the oven to 190°C/375°F/Gas Mark 5.

First, make the gâteaux. Place the chocolate and butter in a bowl and melt them together over a pan of simmering water. Then cool to room temperature. Whisk the eggs, the yolks and the sugar, preferably in an electric mixer or food-processor, until they have doubled in volume, then fold the melted chocolate butter into the egg mix. Sift and fold in the flour. Spoon the mix into the rings or basins, approximately three-quarters full and refrigerate until they are needed, when you will bake them in the preheated oven for 8–9 minutes. Remove the rings (or leave in the bowls) and serve: the centres will still be very soft, sticky and chocolatey.

To make the compôte, stone the cherries and put them in a pan with the syrup and a splash of kirsch, if using. Bring to a simmer and cook for 1–2 minutes. Remove the pan from the heat and strain the liquid from the cherries into another pan. Add the cherry jam to the cherry liquid, bring to a simmer, then strain it immediately on to the cherries: you will have a rich, syrupy cherry compôte. It can be served cold, warm or hot – I prefer it just warm.

To serve, sit the warm sponges on the plates with the warm cherry compôte and spoon the vanilla ice-cream next to them. Place little scrolls/quenelles of clotted cream on top of the sponges and then a chocolate pencil (see page 198) on top of the cream. The clotted cream will just start to melt into the warm gâteaux. When they are cut open, it will then mingle with the melting centres.

Note: A quick cherry compôte can be made with tinned black cherries. Strain off the syrup from the cherries and warm it with cherry jam to give you a good thick rich sauce. Add the cherries and warm through. You may need to use only half of the syrup from the tin.

A few whole cherries can also be used as a garnish to replace the compôte, as shown in the photograph above: these cherries have been dipped in the compôte coulis to give them a rich glaze and flavour.

Valentine Black Forest Heart

Serves 6–8

1 x 35 cm x 25 cm Swiss roll tin,
    buttered and lined with
    greaseproof paper

For the sponge
6 eggs
180 g caster sugar
120 g plain flour
75 g cocoa powder

For the filling (ganache)
375 g plain chocolate, chopped
450 ml double cream
3 tablespoons cherry brandy *or*
    liquor from the Griottine
    cherries (see page 10)
60–75 g Griottine cherries (for
    extra cherry filling use 100 g)

Just because it is called Valentine doesn't mean you can only make this dessert once a year! It is so stunning to look at and even better to taste, that it's worth making at any time. Whenever you serve it, your partner will know it means love!

Preheat the oven to 180°C/350°F/Gas Mark 4.

Whisk the eggs and sugar together in a bowl over simmering water until they form thick ribbons and have doubled in volume. Remove the bowl from the pan and continue to whisk until at room temperature. Sift together the flour and cocoa powder and fold into the egg mixture. Then pour the cake mix into the tin and bake for 8–10 minutes. Remove from the oven and leave to cool.

Melt together the chocolate, half of the double cream and the cherry brandy in a bowl over simmering water. Remove the bowl from the pan and allow to cool slightly. Lightly whip the remaining half of the cream and fold it into the melted chocolate mix. Stir in the cherries. Allow the ganache to cool to a firm but spreadable consistency.

Mix the stock syrup with the cherry brandy.

To build the hearts, turn the chocolate sponge from the tin and remove the paper. Cut in half, giving two 18 x 12.5 cm rectangles. Sit the two rectangles on separate sheets of parchment paper, the 18 cm at the top and 12.5 cm at the sides. Sprinkle each sponge with the cherry brandy syrup. Divide the chocolate ganache between the two, saving 2–3 tablespoons to join them together, spooning and spreading it along the lower half in a wedge shape. Pick up the parchment paper from the top and roll the top half of the sponge onto the wedged ganache. As the sponge and ganache are soft, it can now be gently pushed and moulded into a half heart shape. Repeat for the second half and then refrigerate until completely set.

For the syrup
50 ml stock syrup (see page 188)
50 ml cherry brandy *or* liquor
    from the Griottine cherries

For the garnish
1 quantity warm Cherry Compôte
    from Warm Black Forest
    Gâteau (see page 151)
clotted cream
chocolate pencils (see page 198),
    (optional)

There will still be some of the ganache filling attached to the paper. This is where, once set, we'll be sticking the two half hearts together. While the hearts are setting, they can be moulded again to take on the perfect shape. Once completely firmed, take the halves from the fridge and gently remove the parchment paper. The remaining 2–3 tablespoons of ganache can now be used to join the two together. Simply spread on and attach. Wrap in clingfilm. Return to the fridge, wedging the heart shapes together until completely set, shaping occasionally to take on the perfect heart shape.

Cut the Valentine Black Forest Heart into 2 cm thick slices, using a warmed long sharp (or serrated knife) knife. Lay the heart on a large plate with a scroll or quenelle (see page 11) of clotted cream and a spoonful or two of the cherry compôte. Finish the dish with a chocolate pencil sitting on the clotted cream.

American Cheesecake

Serves 8–10

1 x 25 cm loose-bottomed cake
   tin

1 x 25 cm Genoise sponge (see
   page 197) or 1 ready-made
   vanilla sponge base
225 g caster sugar
3 tablespoons cornflour
750 g full fat soft cream cheese
2 eggs
1 teaspoon vanilla essence
300 ml whipping cream

This is a very famous recipe. But – I have to admit – it's not mine! There's a great bakery/restaurant/café in New York called Junior's, known all over the USA predominantly for its American Cheesecake. Every year they walk away with an award for this recipe.

While I was filming in the States, I spent a day or two at Junior's with them. They told me they've never given away the recipe but after lots of pleading and cajoling, I got hold of it. They've probably left out one little ingredient, but it still tastes great!

At Junior's, it is served either plain or topped with lots of strawberries, chopped nuts and a rich glaze so why not top it with one of the homemade fruit jams featured on pages 193–6?

The sponge base in this recipe is a Genoise. If you make the basic recipe on page 197, the sponge can be sliced into three or four discs and the spares frozen for future cheesecakes. Failing that, buy a vanilla sponge base and cut it to fit.

Preheat the oven to 180°C/350°F/Gas Mark 4.

Butter the cake tin. Cut the sponge horizontally into 1 cm thick discs. Sit one disc in the base of the cake tin (and freeze the others).

Mix together the sugar and cornflour, then beat in the cream cheese, making sure it's blended to a creamy texture. Beat in the eggs and vanilla essence. Then pour on the cream slowly, beating constantly to give a thick, creamy consistency. Now pour the mix on top of the sponge base in the cake tin and smooth over the top. Sit the tin on a baking tray covered about 3 mm deep with warm water. Place in the oven and bake for 45–50 minutes or until the cheesecake is set and golden – check it every 5–10 minutes after the main cooking time. Then remove it from the oven and leave it to cool. Take it out of the tin and it is ready to serve. If it did not colour well in the oven, put it under the grill for a few moments.

At room temperature the American Cheesecake is beautifully soft, rich and creamy. Once it has been refrigerated, the texture becomes almost cakey. I prefer it just cooled, for a softer finish.

Toffee Banana Bread

1 x 900 g loaf tin, greased and
  floured

2 heaped tablespoons toffee
  (see page 187)
4 large bananas, over-ripe
100 g unsalted butter
175 g caster sugar
2 eggs
225 g self-raising flour

This bread is rich in taste and texture. It's not really a bread at all – it got its name from being cooked in a loaf tin – but a toffee and banana cake. The texture is moist and flavoursome. Any slices left over work very well in the Fried Spotted Dick Slice recipe (see page 72) which gives it an even more moist golden-brown finish. As you need the condensed milk toffee for both, why not try it with a scoop or two of the Sticky Toffee Pudding Ice-cream?

Preheat the oven to 180°C/350°F/Gas Mark 6.

Peel and mash the bananas. Beat in the butter and sugar, then the eggs. Mix in the toffee, then the flour. Spoon in the banana mix and bake for 1¼–1½ hours until just firm to the touch. Leave to cool for 10–15 minutes in the tin before turning out.

Mascarpone Champagne Cheesecake

Strawberries go so well with champagne that I like to top this cheesecake with them. However, a soft fruit salad with mango, kiwi, strawberries and raspberries makes a wonderful collection of flavours and colours to enjoy with it too – the choice is yours!

Mix the biscuits with the butter, press into the base of the mould and refrigerate.

Work the mascarpone to a soft creamy consistency. Then whisk the egg yolks, sugar and champagne, including any excess that remains from soaking the gelatine, in a bowl over simmering water until it forms ribbons and doubles in volume. Fold it into the mascarpone. Dissolve the gelatine in a little water and stir it in. Pour the cheesecake mix on top of the biscuit base and leave in the refrigerator to set for 1–2 hours.

Lift the cheesecake out of the tin and peel off the greaseproof paper. Serve with the topping of your choice.

Note: Lemon juice can be used in place of the champagne for Lemon Mascarpone Cheesecake.

Serves 6

1 x 18 cm x 5 cm loose-bottomed cake tin *or* flan ring, lined with greaseproof paper

For the base
200 g digestive biscuits, crumbled
25 g melted butter

For the cheesecake
250 g mascarpone cheese
3 leaves gelatine, softened in a little of the champagne
3 egg yolks
85 g caster sugar
90 ml champagne *or* sparkling wine

Chocolate Prune Cake

Serves 6–8

1 x 20 cm flan/cake tin, buttered and floured

100 g pre-soaked, stoned prunes, chopped roughly
3 tablespoons Armagnac (optional)
200 g caster sugar
4 eggs
200 g unsalted butter
75 g plain flour
75 g cocoa powder
200 g plain chocolate, chopped
75 g chopped pecan nuts
75 g chopped dates

This is a very moreish cake with an abundance of rich ingredients – sure to please everyone! I like to soak the prunes in Armagnac – it's optional, but do put it in – the depth of flavour is just out of this world.

Preheat the oven to 180°C/350°F/Gas Mark 4.

Soak the prunes in Armagnac for 30 minutes. Beat together the sugar and eggs until the sugar has dissolved. Melt the butter and whisk it into the eggs. Sift the flour and cocoa powder into the egg mixture and whisk well. Then melt the chocolate in a bowl over simmering water and add it to the cake mix along with the pecan nuts, dates and prunes – including the Armagnac. Spoon it into the tin and bake for 30–40 minutes until it is just firm. Leave to cool before slicing.

Note: This cake can be served as a dessert, just warm, with a rich Sauce Anglaise (see page 191) or clotted cream.

Battenberg Cake

1 x 20 cm square cake tin, lined with buttered greaseproof paper and divided in half with tin foil

This cake was originally named after the German family who changed their name during the First World War to Mountbatten. The cake's name changed too – to Tennis Cake, due to its resemblance to a tennis court and also because it was served for tea during matches – but not for long. The Battenberg name returned and I'm happy. I've never been much good at serving in tennis!

Preheat the oven to 190°C/375°F/Gas Mark 5.

Beat the butter and sugar in a food-processor until light and creamy. Meanwhile, whisk the eggs in a bowl over simmering water until pale and thick, then add a little at a time to the butter mixture. Sift together the flour and baking powder and fold into the cake mix along with the vanilla essence. Divide the mix in half and add a few drops of colouring to one half. Spoon the cake into the divided cake tin. Bake for 20–25 minutes until just firm to the touch. Leave to cool for 10 minutes before removing from the tin and cooling on a wire rack. Now trim the cake around all the sides, then cut it into four sticks of the same size. Spread the buttercream, jam or both on one side of each cake stick and press them all together so that the two colours are opposite each other. Roll the marzipan on a sugared surface until 2–3 mm thick. Spread more jam or buttercream around the sides of the cake and roll it over marzipan until the cake is covered completely. Trim the excess from each end – the Battenberg is ready to slice!

Note: The marzipan can be given a scaled effect: press a coffee spoon lightly into it in overlapping lines over the whole surface.

225 g unsalted butter

225 g caster sugar

4 eggs

225 g soft plain flour

2 teaspoons baking powder

1 teaspoon vanilla essence

pink food colouring

jam – raspberry, strawberry or apricot

1 quantity buttercream (see page 187)

275 g marzipan (see page 177) *or* bought

Orange Syrup Cake

Serves 12

1 x 25 cm cake tin, lined with
   greaseproof paper, buttered
   and floured

For the cake
225 g butter
225 g caster sugar
4 eggs, beaten
350 g semolina
100 g plain flour
225 g ground almonds
2 teaspoons baking powder
½ litre orange juice

For the syrup
225 g caster sugar
150 ml water
½ litre orange juice

A whole litre of orange juice goes into this cake, half mixed in and half poured over, so it's certainly not short on size or flavour! Plenty of sticky, syrupy, orange cake to fight over!

Preheat the oven to 190°C/375°F/Gas Mark 5.

Cream together the butter and caster sugar until light, pale and fluffy. Beat in the eggs slowly until well incorporated. Mix all the dry ingredients together and add to the butter mix, along with the orange juice. You may find that more orange juice is required to achieve a good dropping consistency. Spread it into the prepared tin and level. Bake for 50–60 minutes until just firm. Remove from the oven and leave to cool before turning out.

Now make the syrup. Dissolve the sugar in the water over a low heat. Add the orange juice and bring to the boil. Simmer for a few minutes then remove from the heat and allow to cool.

To finish, either leave the cake whole or cut into portions. Spoon over some of the syrup and leave it to absorb, then repeat until all the syrup is used. When soaking the whole cake, the syrup will take a little longer to absorb. Serve the Orange Syrup Cake on its own or with pouring cream, extra thick cream, clotted cream, ice-cream, custard, etc., etc., etc. …

Neapolitan Chocolate Mousse

Serves 8–16 (depending on portion size!)

1 x 20 cm square x 7.5–10 cm deep loose-bottomed cake tin, lined with greaseproof paper

1 Fruity Date Cake base, 1 cm thick (see page 164) or 1 Chocolate Genoise (see page 197)

For the chocolate mousses
½ 11 g sachet gelatine granules or 1 leaf
300 ml double cream
150 g chocolate, bitter plain, milk or white, grated
25 ml water
1 tablespoon liquid glucose
1 egg yolk (optional)
cocoa powder for dusting

Neapolitan is usually a combination of three layered ice-creams, strawberry, chocolate and vanilla. Here the three are chocolate: bitter plain, milk and white.

The mousse recipe is for a rich chocolate marquise with a full creamy texture rather than a light airy mousse. Use the same recipe for each of the three mousses, just varying the type of chocolate – and tripling the other ingredients when you do the shopping.

Cut the cake to fit the cake tin and lay it on the base.

Make the bitter plain chocolate mousse first. Soak the gelatine in a little water. Whip the cream to soft peaks. Bring the water and glucose to the boil, then add the chocolate and gelatine. Remove from the heat, beat until the chocolate is smooth and allow to cool. Then stir in the egg yolk, if using – it will enrich the flavour. Fold in the whipped cream and spoon on to the cake base about 2 cm thick. Refrigerate to set. Proceed with the white chocolate mousse, then the milk chocolate mousse. (Any remaining mousse from each batch can be layered in bowls or glasses for extra desserts.) Refrigerate again for 1–2 hours.

Once the pudding has set, warm the outside of the tin and lift out the base. Dust the top with cocoa powder to cover completely, peel off the greaseproof paper and serve.

Note: Bitter Chocolate Sauce (see page 192), Chocolate and Coffee Sauce (see page 192), or Caramel Sauce (see page 192) all complement this dish. It can also be garnished with chocolate pencils or shavings (see page 198), or pipe chocolate directly on to the plate. Make a single-flavoured chocolate dessert by multiplying the mousse ingredients by two or three.

Fruity Date Cake

1 x 20 cm x 7.5–10 cm loose-
  bottomed cake tin, lined with
  greaseproof paper

450 g dates, stoned and
  chopped
450 g raisins
350 g sultanas
275 g butter
275 ml water
1 tin condensed milk (394 g)
300 g plain flour
¾ teaspoon bicarbonate of soda

This cake provides the base to the Neapolitan Chocolate Mousse (see page xx) but if you make it to this quantity, you get double pleasure: number one, you have the base you need, and number two, you're left with an almost complete, very moist fruit cake, that will keep for weeks – if you don't eat it first!

You'll also notice it's a fruit cake made with no eggs – just lots of fruit held together with condensed milk and flour.

Preheat the oven to 170°C/340°F/Gas Mark 3½.

Place the dates, raisins, sultanas, butter, water and condensed milk in a large saucepan and bring to the boil, stirring frequently to prevent it sticking. Once simmering, allow to cook for 3 minutes, stirring occasionally. Remove from the heat, pour into a bowl and allow to cool.

Sift the flour and bicarbonate of soda together and stir into the cake mix. Spoon into the lined cake tin and cover the tin, not making contact with the mix, with tin foil, which will prevent the top burning and becoming too dry. Bake for 1½–1¾ hours until firm to the touch. Remove the tin from the oven and let it stand for 30 minutes before turning out the cake and leaving it to cool. Keep in an airtight container.

Note: If making the Neapolitan Chocolate Mousse (see page 162), the cake will need to be cut 1 cm thick across the bottom to provide the base. Reline the tin with greaseproof paper and sit it in the base, ready for the mousse.

'Iced' Tiramisu

The name of this famous Italian dessert means 'pick-me-up' – and refers to the reviving effect of the coffee it contains! The 'iced' method just gives the pudding a different texture and eats well with the deep chilled effect. It isn't quite frozen, just set very firmly. It's not essential to freeze it at all: chill it in the fridge and you have the classic pudding instead.

Make the mascarpone cream: whisk the egg yolks in an electric mixer or food-processor. While whisking, bring the sugar syrup to the boil, pour gently into the bowl and continue to whisk until the mixture forms ribbons. Add the mascarpone and the Marsala. Pour into a bowl. Whip the cream lightly and fold it into the mascarpone mix.

For the syrup, make the coffee, and while it is hot, stir in the sugar and the Tia Maria. The syrup is ready.

To assemble the Tiramisu, cut the Genoise into 3 horizontally. Place one piece in the base of the tin. Soak with a third of the syrup. Spread over half of the mascarpone cream and sprinkle with half of the grated chocolate then cover with more sponge. Soak with a third of the syrup, cover with the remaining mascarpone, the grated chocolate and top with the last piece of cake. Soak with the coffee syrup and freeze for 1 hour. When ready to serve, remove from the freezer and loosen the cake with a warm knife, or heat the tin carefully with a gas gun (see page 11). Dust the top with cocoa powder and the pick-me-up is ready!

Serves 6–8

1 x 18 cm loose-bottomed cake tin

For the mascarpone cream
4 egg yolks
175 ml stock syrup (see page 188)
200 g mascarpone cheese
250 ml double cream
4 tablespoons Marsala wine

For the syrup
350 ml good strong coffee
100 g caster sugar
50 ml Tia Maria

For the garnish
100 g grated plain chocolate
cocoa powder for dusting

1 x 18 cm Genoise sponge, square or round (see page 197) *or* a bought sponge *or* 1 packet sponge finger biscuits

Iced Sweet Fool

The title doesn't really tell you exactly what is going into this pudding. A fool is a creamy fruit mousse, and with this recipe you can make it almost any flavour, whether using tinned or fresh. So if you decide on peach or apricot, then buy a tin, whiz it to a purée and the job's done! I like strawberry and lemon fool so here it is!

Blitz the strawberries with the lemon juice in a food-processor or liquidizer. Tip into a bowl and fold in the caster sugar. Whip the double cream to soft peaks and fold it into the fruit purée. Spoon the fool into a pudding bowl, smooth the top and freeze for 2–3 hours.

Peel strips of zest from the lemon with a potato peeler. Now cut the long strips into thin strips (julienne) with a sharp knife. Place them in a small saucepan with the water and caster sugar. Bring to a simmer and cook for 1 minute. Leave to cool. Sit the strawberries on top of the frozen fool and decorate each one with a few of the lemon strips. Dust with a little icing sugar through a tea strainer. Now it not only tastes delicious but looks it!

Serves 4

450 g fresh strawberries, washed and stems removed (*or* fruit of your choice)
juice of 1 lemon
50 g caster sugar
150 ml double cream

To decorate (optional)
1 lemon
2 tablespoons water
1 heaped teaspoon caster sugar
8–12 medium strawberries
icing sugar

Petits Fours

Petits Fours are a lovely treat, a bonus at the end of a meal. If you offer a choice, though, you can make a lot of work for yourself, so it's best not to try for more than three. A chocolate truffle, a mini tart, or a marzipan 'fruit' and a tuile or a brandy-snap should be the perfect combination. Or just feature one, a good chocolate truffle, or even fudge.

Whenever you're making chocolates, though, remember: don't try to make them in a hot or humid kitchen, or serve them fridge cold. Remove them from the fridge when they have set and keep them at cool room temperature for a creamy chocolate filling with a crisp outside.

Note: Using a sugar thermometer guarantees the temperature required. If unavailable check the colour required in methods.

Nut Clusters

Makes 30–40 sweets

Best described as roasted, toffeed, caramelised nuts. Yum.

350 g combination of nuts
  (brazil, pecan, unsalted
  peanuts, hazelnuts)
500 ml double cream
25 g butter, cut into small pieces
350 g golden syrup
200 g granulated sugar
75 g soft light brown sugar
15 ml vanilla extract/essence

For a chocolate coating
400 g plain chocolate, chopped
1 tablespoon butter

Roast the nuts in a medium oven for 5–10 minutes until they take on a light golden colour. Leave to cool, then chop roughly.

Put the cream, butter, golden syrup and sugars into a pan over a medium heat, and stir occasionally until the sugar has dissolved. Now bring it to the boil until the temperature reaches 119°C and the caramel is a rich golden brown. Remove the pan from the heat and plunge the base into cold water to stop it from cooking any further. Stir in the vanilla, then the nuts. Oil a spoon and use it to form clusters on oiled parchment paper. Leave to set. To make the chocolate coating, melt the chocolate and butter together in a bowl over a pan of simmering water, then dip each Nut Cluster into the mixture. Leave to harden.

Vanilla Fudge

In a saucepan, mix together the condensed milk, vanilla essence, sugar and butter. Heat gently, stirring occasionally, until the sugar has dissolved and the mixture is smooth. Bring to the boil, and boil until the mixture has turned the classic vanilla golden fudge colour. If using a sugar thermometer this will be at 116°C. Remove from the heat, beat until smooth and pour the fudge into the lined tin. Allow it to cool completely and set before cutting it into squares.

Note: Chopped nuts, raisins or currants can be added to this recipe just before you pour it into the tin.

Makes up to 40 pieces

1 x 20 cm square cake tin, greased and lined with parchment paper

375 g condensed milk
1 teaspoon strong vanilla essence
250 g caster sugar
50 g butter

Chocolate and Pistachio Fudge

The pistachio nuts for this recipe can be chopped or you can blanch them first in boiling water and remove the outer skin. Make the fudge as above, omitting the vanilla. Remove the pan from the heat and beat in the melted plain dark chocolate until smooth. Then stir in the pistachio nuts and pour into the lined tin. Allow the fudge to cool completely and set before cutting it into squares.

Makes up to 50 pieces

1 x 28 cm x 18 cm Swiss roll tin, greased and lined with parchment paper

125 g plain dark chocolate, melted
75 g pistachio nuts, chopped

Pictured overleaf:
Truffles and treats

Filo Pastry

It's an awful lot easier to buy frozen filo pastry; the Greek or Turkish brands tend to be the thinnest. However, I thought that this recipe should be included because it's always fun to have a go at something you thought you'd never touch! But if I was you I'd have a practice on your family before the dinner party ...

Makes approximately 300–350 g

175 ml water
275 g strong plain flour
½ teaspoon salt
25 g melted butter *or* 1
   tablespoon olive oil
cornflour for sprinkling

This pastry is best made in an electric mixer using the dough hook.

Pour the water into a mixing bowl. Add the flour and salt and begin mixing on a low speed. Knead the dough for approximately 10 minutes, then add the melted butter or oil and continue kneading for a further 5 minutes. You will now have a good smooth filo pastry dough. Wrap it in clingfilm and allow it to rest for 30 minutes. To roll, first sprinkle the work surface liberally with cornflour, then start to roll and stretch (you may need to do this in 2–3 batches) into large thin sheets. To maintain an evenly distributed thickness, always stretch the thicker parts first.
Continue until the dough is translucent (as in the picture). Now leave it to dry for a couple of minutes, until it is no longer sticky to touch. Cut into 30 x 40 cm sheets and stack, dusting a little cornflour between each. This will keep refrigerated for 3–4 days or freeze for up to 2 weeks.

Note: The filo can be stacked with greaseproof paper between each layer.

Pastry Cream

Makes approximately 500 ml

4 egg yolks
75 g caster sugar
small pinch of salt
25 g cornflour
300 ml milk
2 vanilla pods, split
35 ml double cream
30 g unsalted butter

A base to many desserts, particularly fruit tartlets and flavoured creams. Try using custard powder instead of cornflour for an even more intense flavour, or for a completely different taste cocoa or instant coffee can take the place of vanilla.

Place the egg yolks, sugar, salt and cornflour in a bowl and whisk until well blended. Bring the milk and vanilla pods to the boil, and whisk into the egg mixture. Transfer the cream back to the pan and place over a medium heat. Stir it constantly until it thickens, 3–5 minutes. Remove the pan from the heat and stir in the double cream and butter.

Strain the pastry cream into a bowl and cover it with lightly buttered greaseproof paper or clingfilm to prevent a skin forming.

Once cooled the cream can be refrigerated for 3–4 days.

Mousseline Cream

Makes 600 ml

4 egg yolks
75 g caster sugar
pinch of salt
75 g cornflour *or* custard powder
300 ml milk
2 vanilla pods, split
125 g unsalted butter

This has the same base as Pastry Cream, but butter is beaten into it, which makes it almost a light and creamy buttercream. It can be used in cakes, pastries or biscuits.

Place the egg yolks, sugar, salt and cornflour in a bowl and whisk until well blended. Bring the milk to the boil with the split vanilla pods and whisk into the egg mixture. Transfer the cream back to the pan and stir constantly on a medium heat for 3–5 minutes until it thickens. Remove from the heat and strain into a bowl. Whisk 25 g of the butter into the cream, cover and leave to cool.

Beat the remaining 100 g of butter slowly in a food-processor for a few minutes to soften it. Then, still beating, add the pastry cream slowly and continue to beat for 5–6 minutes to a light, creamy consistency.

Chantilly Cream

Cream flavoured with sugar and vanilla then whisked to a thick mousse consistency. Don't whisk too much, though, or it will turn into butter. Other flavours can be added, such as the alcohol of your choice or a squeeze of lemon juice. Multiply the ingredients to any quantity you require.

Serves 4–6

150 ml double *or* whipping cream
1 level tablespoon of icing sugar
½ vanilla pod, scraped *or* vanilla essence to taste

Mix all the ingredients together, then taste if using vanilla essence: add more if needed. Now whisk to a creamy mousse consistency. Use immediately.

From left to right: Chantilly Cream, Lemon Vanilla Crème Chiboust and 'Boiled' Buttercream

Lemon Vanilla Crème Chiboust

Serves 6–8

150 ml fresh lemon juice from
    approximately 4–5 lemons,
    plus the grated zest of 2
    lemons
150 ml double cream
4 tablespoons caster sugar
25 g cornflour
6 egg yolks
1 x 11.7 g sachet powdered
    gelatine, soaked in 3
    tablespoons cold water for 5
    minutes
1 vanilla pod, split

For the Italian meringue
200 g caster sugar
50 ml water
6 egg whites

Crème Chiboust is a light pastry cream finished with Italian meringue. Its consistency is so light that if it is not used immediately it may collapse on itself but the gelatine will help prevent that. This does tend to change the consistency slightly, but you will still have a delicious crème. A sugar thermometer is essential for this recipe.

Boil together the lemon juice, zest, vanilla pod and cream. Mix the sugar, cornflour and egg yolks together in a bowl and pour on the boiled juice mix, whisking continually. Return to the pan and cook on a low heat for 8–10 minutes until thickened. Do not allow it to boil. Dissolve the gelatine over a gentle heat until clear and add it to the thickened lemon custard. Strain the custard through a sieve and leave it to cool to tepid.

While the custard is cooling, boil together the water and caster sugar for the Italian meringue, to 121–130°C – it will take 2–3 minutes. While the sugar is boiling, whisk the egg whites to firm peaks. Gradually pour the boiled sugar on to the egg whites, whisking all the time. Then continue to whisk slowly until the meringue is just warm. Fold it into the custard. You can serve the Crème Chiboust straight away, but it can be frozen, which won't spoil the taste or texture. Line a tray or dish 2.5–3 cm deep with clingfilm, pour in the cream and freeze. When you want to eat it, just take it out, cut it into portions and leave it to thaw for a few minutes.

'Boiled' Buttercream

Buttercream is basically just softened butter and icing sugar whisked together to a creamy consistency, with the flavouring of your choice – replace the vanilla here with lemon, orange or whatever you like. 'Boiled' buttercream is a totally different experience – it's what I call real buttercream. It's delicious spread in cakes.

Bring the water and sugar to the boil and cook to soft-ball stage, 117°C. While the sugar is cooking, whisk the egg to double its volume. At soft ball stage allow the sugar to relax for 15–20 seconds, before whisking it slowly into the egg. Continue to whisk until cool. Then beat in the butter a little at a time – this will prevent it from separating – and continue to beat until smooth. Add the vanilla extract and beat again until it is thoroughly blended.

Makes 280 g

50 ml water
125 g caster sugar
1 whole egg
125 g soft unsalted butter
½ teaspoon vanilla extract

Toffee Cream

This is not just a recipe for toffee cream, it also tells you how to make the toffee.

Place the completely unopened tin of condensed milk in a deep saucepan. Cover with cold water, bring to the boil and boil for 3 hours. Keep the tin totally covered with water. After 3 hours remove the pan from the heat and allow the tin to cool while still immersed. The toffee is now ready for use but can be kept refrigerated until the expiry date on the tin. When you open it you will find a rich golden-brown toffee just waiting to be eaten.

For a loose pouring toffee cream simply whisk the cream with the toffee. If you'd prefer a thicker consistency, empty the toffee into a bowl, pour on a quarter of the cream and whisk until thickened. Add another quarter and repeat the same process, continuing until all of the cream has been added.

Note: The ingredients above make a lot of toffee cream. Halve the quantities for a smaller volume.

For the toffee
1 x 200 g tin condensed milk
250 ml double *or* single cream

Candied Syrup Lemons

1–2 large lemons, each cut into 8
  wedges, pips removed
cold water

Good to use as a garnish for many puddings, or with lemon or orange ice-cream.

200 ml water
250 g caster sugar

Place the lemon pieces in a pan, cover with cold water and bring to the boil, then drain off the water and refresh with cold water. Repeat a further four times using fresh water each time. Now bring the sugar and 200 ml of water to the boil. Add the lemon wedges and poach gently for 1½ hours. Leave to cool in the syrup.

Candied Syrup Lemon Strips (julienne)

zest of 2 lemons, peeled
  lengthways

Cut the peel into thin julienne strips. Repeat the same method as above from start to finish, reducing the cooking time to 30 minutes or until tender.

Stock Syrup

Makes 450 ml

You'll find this recipe is referred to throughout the book, used in sorbets, poaching and flavoured syrups.

300 ml water
225 g sugar

Bring the two ingredients to the boil. Simmer for a few minutes until the sugar has completely dissolved and thickened the liqueur. Cool and keep refrigerated.

Fruit Coulis

Makes approximately 500 ml

For red fruit coulis
450 g raspberries *or*
　　strawberries *or* blackberries
100 g icing sugar
85–150 ml water
squeeze of lemon

For other fruit
4 peaches *or* apricots, damsons,
　　plums etc.
100 ml water
2 tablespoons lemon juice
100 g caster sugar

Sweet fruit sauces have become better known as coulis, which means sieved. Classically, you would just sieve the fruit and sweeten with icing sugar. Here the fruit is lightly cooked to break down the texture and give a smooth consistency.

Place all ingredients in a saucepan and heat gently for 5 minutes. Remove from the heat and blend in a food-processor to a purée, then strain through a fine sieve.

Halve and stone the peaches, then chop them roughly. Mix all of the ingredients together and cook on a low heat for 6–7 minutes or until the fruit is tender. Blend to a purée and strain through a sieve.

Note: The coulis flavours can be lifted with the addition of liqueurs to match the fruit, for example, crème de framboises with raspberry. To guarantee a good emulsifying coulis, add a tablespoon or two of jam to the purée before sieving.

Custards and Sauces

Sauce Anglaise (Fresh Custard)

Everybody's favourite sauce.

Beat the egg yolks and sugar together in a bowl until well blended. Pour the milk and cream into a saucepan, add the vanilla pod, then bring it to the boil. Sit the bowl containing the egg mixture over a pan of simmering water and whisk in the boiled cream. Stir until the custard coats the back of a spoon. Remove the bowl from the water and the pod from the custard. Serve warm or cold. To prevent skin forming, cover it with greaseproof paper while it cools.

Note: Don't let this sauce become too hot or the egg yolks will scramble.

Makes 750 ml

8 egg yolks
75 g caster sugar
300 ml milk
300 ml double cream
1 vanilla pod, split (optional)

Variations

Lemon Custard: Add the zest, no pith, of 2 lemons to the milk and cream when heating and leave it in the mix during the whole cooking process. Once the custard has thickened, add the juice of 1 lemon and taste: if the lemon flavour is not strong enough, add more to taste. Strain through a sieve and serve.

Orange Custard: Add the zest of 2 oranges and proceed as for the lemon custard. However, orange juice cannot be used in this recipe so why not add a few drops of Grand Marnier or Cointreau instead.

Rum Custard: Add rum to taste at the end of the cooking process, and a spoonful or two of coconut milk for an extra flavour.

Coffee Custard: Replace the vanilla pod with 2 teaspoons of freshly ground coffee. Once the custard is ready, strain it through a sieve.

Milk Chocolate and Coffee Custard: Proceed as for the Coffee Custard, and grate in 225 g of milk chocolate towards the end of the cooking process.

Chocolate and Coffee Sauce

Makes approximately 500 ml

250 g milk chocolate (plain dark
    will make it even stronger)
175 ml milk
50 ml double cream
125 g unsalted butter
10 teaspoons instant coffee
5 teaspoons hot water

This sauce goes very well with Chocolate Bombe (see page 105). The ice-cream is pretty rich but this sauce will stand up to it.

Dissolve the instant coffee in hot water. Put all the other ingredients into a bowl over a pan of simmering water and melt them together with the coffee. Strain the sauce through a fine sieve and it is ready to serve.

Bitter Chocolate Sauce

Makes approximately 500 ml

300 g bitter dark chocolate,
    chopped
150 g unsalted butter
75 ml double cream

Place all of the ingredients together in a bowl over simmering water until the chocolate has completely melted. Stir well. This sauce is best served warm.

Note: This recipe also works using plain or milk chocolate.

Caramel Sauce

Makes approximately 500 ml

150 ml water
250 g caster sugar
250 ml double cream

Pour the water into a saucepan with the caster sugar. Stir with a spoon to mix and then leave on a low heat until the sugar has dissolved. Now turn up the heat and cook the sugar to caramel stage. During this time you may find some of the sugar crystallising around the edge of the pan. If so, wash it away with a pastry brush dipped in cold water. If you have a sugar thermometer, you need to heat the mixture to 158°C. If not cook it to a rich golden brown.

While the sugar is caramelising, warm the cream. When the caramel is ready, remove the pan from the heat and leave it for 10–15 seconds before pouring on the cream slowly. Once all the cream has been added, return the pan to the heat and simmer the sauce for 5 minutes. Strain it through a fine sieve.

Caramel Port Sauce: Follow the recipe above and add approximately 6 tablespoons of port – simply delicious!

Homemade Fruit Jams, Marmalades and Sauces

This recipe applies to soft fruit such as raspberries, strawberries, blackberries, cherries, tayberries, loganberries, blackcurrants, etc., but will work with large soft fruit such as ripe plums, peaches and apricots. All of them, apart from strawberries, cherries and peaches, hold a medium amount of pectin, the natural substance found in the cells of fruit. This is then released by the natural acids also present in the fruit. Cooking the fruit in sugar releases the pectin and forms the setting jelly.

The proportion of sugar to fruit is important in jam-making: the normal ratio is equal quantities of either, which helps the pectin to reach setting point and preserves the jam. However, in this recipe, the quantity of sugar is half that of the fruit: sugar with added pectin gives a jellied syrup, with a much looser consistency than jam, almost like thick sauce, and the fruit flavour is not over-sweetened. It doesn't have the shelf life of a 'real' jam, but kept refrigerated it will last for several months.

All the small soft fruit should be used whole, except larger strawberries which can be halved. Cut plums, apricots and peaches into large wedges.

Raspberry Jam

Place the sugar, zest and lemon juice into a large pan and bring to a simmer. Add the raspberries and stir in carefully. Bring the mix to the boil, skimming off any impurities, and boil for just 3–4 minutes. Remove the pan from the stove and again remove any impurities. You now have a good, rich, shiny jam, with the raspberries still holding some shape. Leave to cool slightly, then spoon into containers or warm sterilised (see Note) jam jars. Seal, label and keep refrigerated, or if making the jam with equal quantities of fruit and sugar, keep in a cool place, where it will last almost indefinitely.

Note: To sterilise the jars, place them in a large saucepan, cover with cold water, bring it to the boil and boil for 15 minutes. Carefully remove and leave to dry. Once the jars have been filled, covered and sealed, you can sterilise again: sit the jars on a wire rack or cloth in a large pan and almost cover them with water. Bring to the boil and boil for 15 minutes. Remove from the pan, dry and cool.

Makes 750 g

450 g jam sugar
finely grated zest and juice of
½ lemon
900 g fresh raspberries

Orange Marmalade

Makes 1.25–1.5 kg

450 g oranges
juice of 1 lemon
1.2 litres water
900 g granulated sugar *or*
  preserving sugar

The best oranges to use, for their strong bitter flavour and high pectin content, are Seville, in season from late December/early January until late February. However, almost any orange and other citrus fruit – lemon, lime, grapefruit – can be used in this recipe. How did marmalade get its name? There are several stories! Until the seventeenth century, marmalade was made from quince, known in Spain and Portugal as marmalada *and* mamelo, *hence the name 'marmalade'. Later oranges took the place of quince, but the name stayed the same. Another story I read was about the voyage of Mary, Queen of Scots, from France to Scotland to claim her throne. She was seasick, and one of her maids, who was making a dish of bitter oranges for her, said, 'Marie est malade', which sounds a bit like marmalade. Who knows?*

The pectin in citrus fruits is held in the pith and pips so we shouldn't throw them away. The sugar content in marmalade is double that of the fruit, to balance the bitterness of the peel.

Wash and scrub the oranges to remove any artificial colouring. Halve them and squeeze out the juice, keeping any pips and membrane. Now cut the orange shells in half and cut away the pith. This really depends on how bitter you prefer your marmalade to be. Put it with the pips and membrane in a piece of muslin, discarding the rest and tie it into a bag. Cut the peel into thin or thick strips and place it in a saucepan with the lemon juice and the water. Tie the bag to the pan handle and submerge it in the water.

Bring it to a simmer and cook for 1–1½ hours, until the peel is tender and the liquor has reduced by half. Remove the muslin bag, squeezing out any juices and discard it.

Add the sugar and stir over a low heat until it has dissolved. Now bring the marmalade to the boil, skimming away any impurities and stirring from time to time. Cook for 10 minutes. While the marmalade is boiling chill a side plate, for testing the setting point. After 10 minutes has passed, spoon a little marmalade on to the plate and chill. It should jellify and

wrinkle when moved with a spoon, but if it does not, continue to boil for a further 5 minutes and retest. Remove from the heat and skim off any impurities. Leave to stand for 15–20 minutes. Stir it to spread the peel, then ladle into sterilised jars (see Note, page 193). Cover and seal. Store in a cool, dark area.

Note: 50–60 ml of either brandy, whisky, Cointreau or Grand Marnier can be added at the end of the cooking time; or why not put in 50–75 g of freshly grated ginger with the orange peel for a spicy finish.

Lemon Curd

Makes approximately 750 g

225 g caster sugar
225 g unsalted butter
finely grated zest and juice of 3 lemons
5 egg yolks

Delicious on toast, crumpets or scones. I often make the lemon-curd base for the ice-cream on page 86 from this recipe. This lemon curd will also give you a good thick lemon sauce to go with a steamed sponge. Use 100 g of butter and 3–4 egg yolks for a less rich lemon curd with a slightly more fluid consistency.

Put the sugar, butter, lemon juice and zest in a bowl and stir over a pan of simmering water. Once the butter has melted, beat vigorously until well mixed. Beat in the egg yolks and continue to cook for 15–20 minutes until the curd has thickened. Pour into a clean jar and cover with waxed paper or clingfilm. If kept refrigerated the lemon curd will last for up to two weeks.

Note: For Orange Curd, substitute 3 oranges for the lemons. Boil the juice to reduce it by half. You could add a little Grand Marnier or Cointreau, which will intensify the flavour.

Vanilla Sponge (Genoise)

A basic recipe that can form the base of gâteaux, trifles and many other puddings. Make the vanilla-flavoured syrup from caster sugar in which one or two vanilla pods have been kept.

This recipe fills a 20 cm round or square cake tin. For a 15 cm tin, halve the recipe. If you need only a 1 cm cake base for a pudding, make the whole recipe, wrap what you don't need in clingfilm and freeze.

1 x 20 cm round *or* square cake tin, lined with buttered greaseproof paper

6 eggs
175 g caster sugar (preferably flavoured with vanilla)
175 g plain flour
50 g butter, melted

Preheat the oven to 200°C/400°F/Gas Mark 6.

Whisk the eggs and sugar together in a bowl over a pan of hot water until they have doubled in volume and become light and creamy. Remove from the heat and continue to whisk until cold and thick, forming ribbons. Lightly fold in the flour and melted butter. Pour the mix into the prepared tin and bake for 30–40 minutes. Test with a skewer, which will come out clean when the sponge is ready. Allow to cool for 10 minutes in the tin, then turn out on to a wire rack.

Note: The sponge can be split and spread with jam (see page 193) and whipped cream, then dusted with icing sugar to give you a Victoria Sponge. For Chocolate Genoise replace 25 g of the flour with 25 g of cocoa powder.

Chocolate Pencils and Shavings

For the pencils
100 g chocolate, plain, milk *or* white

For the shavings
225 g chocolate, plain, milk *or* white

Chocolate is such a workable substance. The variety of shapes that can be formed is almost unlimited, and they make any pudding look even more appetising.

Take 2 baking sheets – any size will do. Clean well, then warm them to approximately 50°C/120°F, then lay them base up on the work surface. Run the chocolate, whole, slowly up and down the tray in even lines. This will allow it to melt, leaving a thin, even coat covering the tray. Once both trays are coated leave them in a cool place to set, the refrigerator will do, but the chocolate must be allowed to come back to room temperature before you attempt to pencil. If it is too hard it will crumble rather than roll.

For perfect pencils you will need a metal pastry scraper, around 10 cm wide. Push the scraper between the chocolate and the baking sheet, using short rapid movements, which will produce thin pencil shapes. When you have finished, place the trays in the fridge to set the chocolate then lift the pencils carefully from the tray, and keep them in a suitable container in the freezer. Because they are so thin it's best to use them directly from the freezer. The chocolate defrosts very quickly. One or two per portion will be plenty.

The shavings are very easy to make and should also be kept in the freezer. The chocolate should come from at least a 225 g block. Once opened, leave it to come to room temperature. Then hold a metal 5 cm diameter pastry cutter or ring at a 30°–45° angle to the chocolate, pull on the chocolate and the shavings will appear. Continue until all the chocolate is used (any trimmings will just have to be eaten!). Place the shavings in the freezer until needed.

Note: It's important when working the chocolate that the shapes are made in a cool room.

Cheesy Biscuits

I love cheese, and I like to offer it before or after dessert, so I've included a few savoury recipes for biscuits to accompany it. These will all keep well for a few days in an airtight container. You'll notice a recipe for home-made digestives that also go well with cheese – or just for dunking in tea.

Note: When you are rolling and cutting biscuits, trimmings will be left over. Press them together and roll out again to cut a few more. One or two rollings are enough; after that the dough becomes overworked and the biscuits chewy.

Oatmeal Biscuits

Preheat the oven to 180°C/350°F/Gas Mark 4.

Mix together the flour, oatmeal, salt and baking powder, then rub in the butter to give a crumbly texture. Now work in the water and knead to a biscuit dough. Either wrap in clingfilm and refrigerate for use later, or roll it out on a lightly floured surface until it is 3 mm thick. Now cut out the biscuits with a 5 cm round cutter and place them on a baking tray, lined with parchment or other baking paper. Bake for 12–15 minutes. Leave to cool a little, then transfer to a wire rack.

Makes approximately 45–50

125 g plain flour, sifted
250 g fine oatmeal
pinch of salt
2 teaspoons baking powder
125 g butter, diced
60 ml boiling water

Wholemeal Biscuits

Preheat the oven to 180°C/350°F/Gas Mark 4.

Mix together the wholemeal flour, salt and baking powder. Then rub in the butter to give a crumbly texture. Work the milk and egg into the mixture until you have a dough. It can now be covered in clingfilm and kept refrigerated until needed, or roll it 3 mm thick and cut it into 5 cm rounds.

Place the biscuits on a baking sheet lined with parchment or other baking paper and bake for 15–18 minutes. Leave to cool a little, then transfer to a wire rack.

Makes approximately 40–45

250 g wholemeal flour
1 teaspoon salt
2 teaspoons baking powder
90 g butter, diced
5 teaspoons of milk
1 whole egg, beaten

199

Water Biscuits

Preheat the oven to 180°C/350°F/Gas Mark 4.

Mix together the flour, baking powder and salt. Rub in the butter to a crumbly texture. Add the water and mix to a dough. It can now be wrapped in clingfilm and refrigerated until needed, or roll it 2 mm thick. Cut out rounds 6 cm in diameter. Place the biscuits on a baking sheet lined with parchment or other baking paper and prick each one with a fork. Bake for 15–20 minutes until they are crispy. Transfer the biscuits on to a wire rack and leave to cool.

Note: A baking tray can be placed on top of the biscuits for the first 7–10 minutes for a thinner biscuit.

Makes approximately 35–40

375 g plain flour, sifted
2 teaspoons baking powder
1 teaspoon salt
90 g butter, diced
140 ml water

Digestive Biscuits

Delicious on their own or with cheese – and, of course, you can break them up and mix the crumbs with melted butter for a cheesecake base. But I'm not sure that I'd go to the trouble of making them just to smash them to bits!

Preheat the oven to 180°C/350°F/Gas Mark 4.

Mix all the dry ingredients together. Rub in the butter until the mixture binds. Now add the milk and work to a pliable dough.

Roll it out on a lightly floured surface to 3 mm thick and cut it into approximately 6 cm diameter discs. Lay the biscuits on a greased baking tray and prick each one with a fork. Bake for 12–15 minutes or until golden brown, then remove from the oven and allow to cool for a few minutes, and transfer to a wire rack.

They will stay crisp and fresh for a few days kept in an air-tight container.

Makes approximately 30

150 g wholemeal flour
50 g plain flour
50 g fine oatmeal
1 teaspoon baking powder
pinch of salt
2 tablespoons soft light brown sugar
100 g butter
4 tablespoons milk

Chocolate

Chocolate was first brought to Europe by the Spanish, who discovered the cocoa tree in Mexico in 1519. The plant, however, is believed to have grown in the New World for around 4,000 years. Cocoa beans form in large pods (30–40 almond-sized beans per pod) on the tree – *Theobroma cacao*, *Theobroma* meaning 'food of the gods'.

Each pod is cut from the tree with a machete to ensure that no damage is done to the tree, which might lead to disease. Then the pods are split, revealing fleshy white fruits, which are placed in vats and allowed to ferment. The fleshy surround falls off leaving light brown cocoa beans. The beans are dried, preferably in sunlight. However, they can also be oven dried, although this can result in a smoky flavour. Top manufacturers – in particular, Valrhona, the specialist producer in the Rhône valley, France – will not accept any beans that have been oven-dried.

Once the beans reach the chocolate factory, they are roasted to develop their flavour. Beans from different plantations must all be roasted separately: each variety carries its own flavour and is roasted to a different stage so that when they are blended with others the right depth of flavour and bitterness will be achieved. As many as 10 or 12 varieties of bean are used by some chocolate-makers to find the right balance.

Chocolate-making has a close similarity to wine production. In wine, mixing and creating a cuvée basically means blending grapes to make the right wine. The same rule applies to chocolate. The other term common to both industries is '*cru*', which means growth: a good champagne will claim '*grand cru*', and Valrhona were the first to produce '*grand cru*' chocolate, from a plantation producing the finest cocoa beans. They maintain the excellence of this product by employing 12 expert tasters to check its quality daily. Lucky experts!

After roasting, the bean skins are removed, leaving the kernel. It takes several processes to turn the dried cocoa beans into chocolate. Now the chocolate-making begins. The kernels are passed through giant rollers to crush until ground. Two more stages follow. First, either the crushed kernels can be pressed, which melts the cocoa butter, leaving behind cocoa powder – a product we all enjoy. This process is normally carried out by a large manufacturer, who needs the extra cocoa butter to produce a quality chocolate. The other method is to grind the kernels to a paste, which is then mixed with extra cocoa butter, sugar and vanilla to make chocolate, which is ground again for anything from one to five days. The longer it's ground the smoother and silkier the chocolate becomes. This method is known as conching. So, basically chocolate has two main components: cocoa solids (this contains cocoa butter) and sugar.

Chocolate with a cocoa solid content of 85 per cent or over is considered unpalatable as it is too bitter. The best range is from 55 per cent to 75 per cent and should hold 31 per cent cocoa butter. If there is less than 50 per cent of cocoa solids in plain chocolate, the rich flavour will be lacking.

Extra bitter chocolate ranges from 75 per cent to 85 per cent cocoa solids. This is palatable but strong. A bitter chocolate will be in the 55 per cent to 75 per cent range. The Valrhona 'Grand Cru', which falls into this category, is probably the best for cooking. A less sweet chocolate will yield a fuller, rich chocolate taste and to balance the bitterness more sugar can be added to the dessert. There are also bitter-sweet and semi-sweet chocolates: the bitter-sweet varieties must always include a minimum of 35 per cent cocoa solids. 'Couverture' chocolate we use in the industry contains 31 per cent cocoa butter within the solids, which makes it easier to work with. I have always bought my cooking chocolate from Valrhona, and Callebaut, a famous Belgian company, well respected for its chocolate.

A chocoholic's dream

These makes are not always easily obtainable, but Lindt, the Swiss chocolate, is readily available and good to work with.

In continental Europe, milk chocolate is mostly made with condensed milk. In Britain and the USA a 'milk crumb' (milk and sugar) mixture is used, along with cocoa, cocoa butter and sugar. It should hold at least 31 per cent fats and only ever contain a maximum of 55 per cent sugar.

White chocolate is a blend of cocoa butter, sugar and milk, and, for a quality product, should contain no more than 50 per cent sugar.

So, summing up my feelings about chocolate, if you want to achieve the maximum flavour from any of the desserts featured here, or anywhere else for that matter, always use the best chocolate available. This will mean spending a little more – but enjoying an awful lot more.

Chocolate doesn't just melt on its own, it takes you with it.

Liqueurs and More

Amaretto
Almond and apricot kernels
Italy

Cointreau
Oranges (bitter orange rind)
France

Grand Marnier
Oranges
France

Crème de Cassis
Blackcurrant
France

Crème de Framboise
Raspberry
France

Crème de Menthe
Mint
France

Frangelico
Hazelnut
Italy

Maraschino/Kirsch
Cherry
Italy

**Poire William/
  Eau de Vie de Poire**
Pears
France

Liqueurs

Best described as an after-dinner alcoholic drink with strong fruit, berry or other flavours added.

And more ...

Armagnac is a French brandy with a history that goes back over five hundred years (that's two hundred more than brandy itself!). Its name, Armagnac, may only be used on brandy made in an area within the ancient province of Gascony. Armagnac has a full-bodied earthy, nutty flavour with a slight hint of prunes.

Cognac is a white grape-based alcohol, made from several varieties, the main being St Emilion, named after its region. The difference between wine and brandy is that Cognac is distilled after fermentation. After fermentation, and with a special yeast, the grapes are cooked over a wood fire. Distillation is performed twice. The first resulting at 28 per cent alcohol, the second 70 per cent. This leaves it colourless and obviously very strong. The next step is to age, refine and mature in oak barrels before it is ready to drink.

Calvados is made from apple cider in Normandy, France. Aged in oak for at least two to five years, it matures slowly and is bottled at between 80 and 86 per cent proof.

Bailey's was invented in 1779 by R. & A. Bailey and Co. Ltd of Dublin. It became a best-selling liqueur throughout the world: over a million cases are produced each year. A major ingredient of all Irish cream liqueurs is milk, Bailey's included. It has a coffee-cream flavour.

Sherry takes its name from the Spanish fortified wine Xeres which is produced principally from the Palomino grape. Sherry varies in colour and flavour, from pale gold – very dry, to dark brown – sweet.

Marsala a distant cousin of sherry, found in the region of Sicily that bears the same name.

Sauternes is a sweet white wine from the Bordeaux region of France.

Index

Abraham Hayward, QC, in *The Art of Dining*, 1852, says:

'The late Lord Dudley could not dine comfortably without an apple pie, as he insisted on calling it, contending that the term tart only applied to open pastry. Dining with the Foreign Secretary, at a grand dinner at Prince Esterhazy's, he was terribly put out on finding that his favourite delicacy was wanting, and kept on murmuring pretty audibly, in his absent way: "God bless my soul! No Apple Pie."'

Taken from *Good Things in England*,
ed. Florence White
(Jonathan Cape/The Cookery Book Club 1968)